TIPTOE

ISBN 978-0-9934693-0-5

Designed and typeset by Carnegie Book Production, Carnegie House,
Chatsworth Road, Lancaster LA1 4SL

Printed in the UK by Jellyfish Solutions

Contents

The Edge of the World

THERE WAS ONCE A LITTLE BOY who dreamed of being a knight. He played with a plastic sword in his mother's garden. He cantered around on his imaginary horse, searching for dragons to slay. At the end of the garden near the pond he saw a dragon jumping around. It was green and wet and stared at him with round bulging eyes. He squashed it under his foot. No-one wanted to play knight games with him. All the boys played football and the girls didn't need to be rescued. So he killed dragons by himself.

One winter night when the boy was asleep, dreaming heroes' dreams, a dragon crawled under his door and climbed up his duvet. It scurried over his arm and chest and neck. It was so small he could have squished it with two fingers. The dragon bit into the boy's skin and sipped until its little dragon tummy was full and then crawled back down the duvet and into the shadows under the bed.

When the boy awoke he felt far-away. His neck was hurting but the mark was too small to see. The extra drops didn't show on his pillow because everyone knows a dreamer's blood runs white like the pages of a storybook. On his way home from school the next day he chased a dragon down an alleyway until it pranced up onto a wall and out of sight. Another dragon barked at him from across the street but he was too tired to chase again. His mother yelled at him for being late; she tried, but she wasn't a real dragon.

After supper and story time he went to sleep. Later, when the house was hushed, the dragon crawled out again. It scuttled along the floor and up the duvet. Tonight it was hungrier; it drank the boy's milky storybook blood until its little stomach was swollen. Then it crawled back into the shadows. In the morning the boy was further away. His mother laughed, thinking toast and tea would bring him back. At school the boy had given up asking others to join his games. He was happy alone with his imaginary horse. He killed a dragon as it scurried up the bark of a sycamore tree.

From then on, every day, the little boy woke up further away while under his bed the dragon was growing bigger. Its eyes were white and its limbs were jagged and grey. Sometimes in between dreams the boy would hear a scuttling or a dry rasp of breath but never enough to make a memory.

The boy grew up strong and sad and gentle and he packed his bag and left the town. He told his mother she would understand him eventually and he cantered off into the forest on his imaginary horse. Somewhere between the rainy days he saw it, in a clearing, scales gleaming in the sunlight. It had grown since the nights it used to hide beneath his bed. It was jagged and grey and monstrous and when its wings beat the treetops rippled. Before he could draw his sword it was gone. He galloped through the trees, backpack bouncing behind him, but the dragon was nowhere to be seen. That night, as he drifted into a troubled sleep, he swore he would find it again, if he had to travel to the ends of the earth.

The next day he chewed on his biscuit breakfast. All the carrots were rotten so the horse had biscuits too. From dawn he walked until the sun was too far gone to see his path, and so it was every day. And every night he watched the stars and dreamed his troubled dreams. He walked to the end of the forest, through dust and open sky, dizzied by the sun. Through strange towns filled with watchful eyes and silent prayers. Then one day, when his face was thick with frowns and whiskers, he reached the ends of the earth. There he dismounted, laid down his backpack and crept to the edge. Beyond it and below, the emptiness was white like the pages of a storybook.

He camped there that night and gazed along the barren horizon at all the figures tiptoeing alone along the edge of the world. Some had their arms outstretched, like tightrope walkers; others knelt peering over the ledge, touching the emptiness with their fingertips. From time to time he thought he saw the grey outline of distant wings against the white, barely bigger than a speck of dust. When morning came he stood up, holding the hilt of his sword. There was no dragon to be seen. Testing the ground with each step, he approached. The other tiptoers all along the horizon watched as he placed the first foot over the edge of the world. And then the second. It was like walking over snow and making no foot prints.

"Do I know this story?"

It crawled closer and craned its neck. *Don't you want to hear the ending?*

1

Knight

ROAN'S ALARM CLICKED. Clicking was better than ringing, less intrusive, enough to wake but not to startle. Keeping his body as still as he could, he extended a hand and turned it off. With the same hand he picked up his notebook and pen:

- *Snowing*
- *White photographs*
- *Voyeur*
- *Can't move*

He wrote with the book up above his chest. Movement speeds up the forgetting. Lying still will buy you another thirty seconds, before the haze comes in.

It gave him chills. Not a nightmare, more like the answer to a riddle, or a half-formed memory. He twisted out of bed and replaced the book on the nightstand. It was five a.m. He pulled the cord of the blind and felt the light swimming over him. The sun dispelled the last of the dreams. He looked back over the bullet points; all their meaning was gone.

It took a few minutes to open his eyes fully. Then he moved to the sink and splashed water over his face and hair. The mirror was too low for him but he stooped a few inches just to see the dripping from his chin. His own gaze burned into him. Roan's gaze burned into everyone. His forehead and cheeks were sombre, whatever expression he tried to pull. Water ran down clumps of long hair, over his face and through the hairs on his chest. He opened the window to let the breeze dry him. It was going to be hot again today.

Outside, the street was still but for a suited man trudging through leaves. Roan watched, then pretended to fix the blind when the man looked up. His clothes were squashed in one corner behind the bed. On the far side by the kitchen worktop was a single threadbare sofa and all the grocery shopping he had forgotten to pack away. The floor was covered with ankle-height paper sculptures. He stepped carefully around them as he got dressed. The walls were empty and stained with damp. He hated hot days: his armour absorbed the sun and cooked him slowly. Once he had fainted – fallen backwards onto the pavement. When he inspected it that night, his body plate had a dent. He must have clanged.

For breakfast he made a spaghetti hoop sandwich and slurped a few mouthfuls of water from the tap. Before he left he perched on the end of the sofa to tweak the little structures on the floor, nudging a stray building back in line with the street. A neighbour greeted him in the corridor, catching him off guard so he responded too late. His armour was jangling in a holdall by his leg. About this time every morning, as he went into the outside air, Roan had the same feeling. A hollowness in his chest, a tame sorrow. It would be gone within the hour.

He wasn't a street mime; he had evolved beyond that. He didn't move or act or entertain. It was not about pleasing people. It was half-past six when he parked up and wriggled his body into the armour. He never enjoyed the walk from his car; it was too noisy and broke the illusion. Today no one noticed as he arrived and settled in position, locking into the familiar stance as though he had been there all night.

The helmet had a visor that pointed outwards like a snout and slits just wide enough to watch the passing heads and shoulders. People studied him as they walked to work. Most had seen him before and gave only a passing glance. Some dropped money into the cup by his feet. Others treated him like a real statue. He would be here until after the evening rush hour. Between now and then he had nothing but empty time and peace. First he deepened his breaths, feeling calmer with every exhale, then he let his eyelids droop. A few more breaths and it would all disappear.

"YAAAAAAAAAGH!"

Roan jumped to life. The yell was urgent and right by his ear.

"Aha! You are a coward!" Turning round he saw a familiar toothy grin. In a swift motion the man moved a few paces away, looking him up and down. *"Good Morning Pepper? No? Or a salute maybe?"*

Roan re-adopted his pose.

"You in there? I know, I know, you're in character. One of these days I'll come by and speak to an empty suit, while you're at home having a lie-in. Aha. Anyway! I know you don't want to speak, so you can listen. Guess what I have today. Don't say it, just guess. You see I'm bored of performing tricks every day, so I'm mixing it up. Merchandising. Building a little magic for people to take home for £25 a pop … Guessed yet? I'll tell you: FLAMING WALLETS! I'll show you."

He drew a black leather wallet from his pocket and held it up. Then he opened it slowly, revealing the cards and notes inside. "Ordinary wallet, for an ordinary man." He was dressed in a dark blue suit, the shoulder pads protruding sideways from his gangly body. "You're not an ordinary man though are you, Mr Knight-in-shining-armour?" A quizzical smile rode up one cheek toward the end of each sentence. He was tanned and skeletal, the top of his beard cut off abruptly into a bald head. "Ha. Of course not. Ordinary men answer questions. You ignore them. So maybe you are an extraordinary man."

Pepper spun around to intercept a passing woman. "Hey! Hey … Hey! Oi!" He stretched his head towards her. The woman shuffled quickly past, ignoring the intrusion. "I'm quite the sales man, I've discovered. Not today though, I'm not on form today. She looked sharp. Talking to her would've put me back on form. But I wasn't on form enough to talk to her. A pickle." His speech was emphatic and raspy. "Anyway, watch this. Pretend you're a woman. And pretend I'm you, and you wanna impress. It's not enough to be chivalrous these days." He drove his hand towards Roan's chest with a grasping motion, pretending to pull out his heart, then brought it back and examined the invisible heart, sniffed it and slotted it into the wallet. Roan watched silently. Pepper shook the wallet and kissed it. With a final flourish he flipped it open, releasing a torrent of flames. They flurried upward past his nose sending wisps of grey smoke into the air. For a few seconds they both admired, then the wallet snapped shut and the flames were gone. "That's what love would look like. A living stage play. Or maybe it's just a flame. It sends mixed messages and that's the language women speak in, isn't it? I think you could get yourself a few lady friends, a few damsels with this party piece, wouldn't you agree?" While performing, Roan rarely acknowledged anyone, no matter how intrusive they were. Once a child had stuck an ice cream cone on his nose; he just waited for it to fall off. "The thing is," Pepper continued, "there are separate flaps inside. One contains the ordinary wallet interior, for all your notes and cards and damsel pictures. The other one contains a liquid capsule you can fill with ordinary lighter fluid. No leakage. And you have to open it vigorously to fire the ignition. So no unexpected accidents. Only £25. How does that sound Mr Knight?" Pepper's keen eyes cut through the gaps in the helmet, probing Roan patiently.

After a few seconds Roan cleared his throat, unable to bear his own silence. "I don't really need a wallet." The helmet distorted his voice sending the words back to his own ears.

"Eh?"

"I…I don't need a wallet. I haven't got any money on me…to buy it with."

The lopsided smile returned in vague disbelief. "Aha. Aha. He speaks. He lives. I know you don't want one boyo, I'm practising my pitch. Made 'em myself – what do you think?"

"It's a clever idea."

"Glad you think so. Now, seeing as you're awake, I'll throw in a free sachet of lighter fluid."

"Like I say, I'm…"

"You pay me fifty pounds for the wallet plus you get a free twenty five pounds and you get to keep the wallet and the extra money and the sachet. If you pay me tomorrow, I'll be back. I'll give you the wallet then. Aha!" He punched the breast plate playfully. "Aha! Only joking. Confusion tactics – effective in magic, not effective in sales – make people think you're a nut. Now listen here, I want to see you tomorrow. Come by the office and don't tell me you have plans … And bring fifty pounds. Aha!" Pepper glanced around, slid the wallet back in his pocket and moved across the road with spidery strides. Roan remained stock still in position, his warm breath oozing against the inside of the helmet, dampening his hidden face.

2

The Hospital

ON HIS FIRST VISIT ROAN had paced the street for nearly twenty minutes before knocking. While he sat in the waiting room, she had examined him from behind her desk, eyes bulging unpleasantly. Roan had scowled back at her, not sure why. She was young but weathered, with dark hair squeezed into a bun. For a few seconds they said nothing and then she introduced herself as Ms Limms. Roan found it hard to look at her. When she brought him a coffee, he regretted scowling and tried to make conversation. She told him she had worked for Mr Hansel ever since leaving school, he was a pleasure to work for, when he wanted to be. The room was a dirty cream colour, with thinning brown carpet and solemn paintings on the wall. He wondered what a street magician needed a secretary for, but he didn't ask. Years later and nothing had changed but the lines on Ms Limms' face.

Roan flinched, looking up from the arm of the chair he'd been picking at. "Sorry, what did you … ?"

"Mr Hansel is ready to see you," Ms Limms repeated. Thanking her, he moved towards the door marked *Pepper's Room – No girls allowed.*

"Roan."

"Hello Pepper."

"How is my artist?" Pepper was dressed in a woollen jumper and the worn-out expression he kept for the indoors.

"I'm fine, good."

"You're an artist, you can't be fine. Artists are a-flame with tears and confusion, no?"

"I'm trying not to be too a-flame, everything's a bit easier when …"

"Aha, of course. I have flames on the brain."

The floor was strewn with piles of books, half drawn diagrams and props from his show, devices made of wood and mirrors on hinges. There was even a black top hat, which Roan had never seen outside the office. The window looked onto a glass tower block across the street and the pigeons huddled on the lampposts.

"Now," Pepper began limply, "when's the next masterpiece? May I ask?"

"I'm trying a few different acts, no masterpiece yet."

"You'll know when it comes along. It'll kick down your door; it won't ring the bell like the rest." Pepper's face was sour, between the occasional smiles.

"I'll keep at it."

"I hope you will." He stretched his fingers back against each other. "You're out there to make a masterpiece, not just to stand around in funny clothes. We've got Ms Limms for that."

"For what?"

"Exactly!" he barked, animated again. "She's a ghost in the machine. You know who said that, don't you? Gilbert Ryle, the philosopher. Not about Ms Limms of course." Roan laughed self-consciously. "You know what my father told me?"

"What was that?"

"He said one day everyone will be descended from a sperm donor. So learn to recognise greatness before it's gone and we all become wankers. That's what I'm doing with you." Roan looked up at the mini chandelier, choosing his words. Before he could speak Pepper sighed and scratched his neck. "You want a drink Roan, don't you? You don't want me thinking I'm going senile with all this enthusiasm, do you?"

"I could have a small drink."

"Of course you could, not too much or Ms Limms will tell on us. And you know who she'll tell, don't you?"

"Who?"

"Plants, that's who, in her flat. Tells them everything, she reckons it helps them grow. Mind you, with all the complaining she does it's a wonder they don't walk out." In the corner of the room was a small table, covered in bottles. "I'm going to give you whisky because there's tiptoe mixed into some of the other bottles and I can't remember which ones. Unless you want an extra boost?"

"No thanks, I don't…"

"Noble fellow." He returned with two glasses. "Some people get hooked on every pleasantry life offers them. Cheers." They touched glasses, briefly quiet again but for Pepper slurping. "So tell me Roan, what *is* your chosen vice? Don't tell me. I know already. That faraway look you have. What else could your vice be? Aha. So how's it coming along then?"

"How's what coming along?"

"The mourning."

Roan gave a non-committal nod. There was a sinking in his chest that may have been shame. He watched the slurred reflections of passing traffic in the windows across the street.

"Roan, I think I'm ready to take you on that visit."

In the passenger seat, Roan tried to read the graffiti as it sped past.

"It's like the archaeology channel out here," Pepper was saying. "Some city it's become, eh? I don't suppose we call it city? Not organised is it? Not a community. This is just brick-a-brack, like a garage sale … Garage sale for government oafs." Rundown industrial estates appeared at intervals between patches of grassland, many were derelict, their smoky coloured bricks strung with climbing plants. Occasionally Roan would spot piles of rubble and weeds where smaller houses had long ago been destroyed and overgrown. "I'm not a whiner though, Roan. When I'm an old man I'll be the less annoying type. If I have grandchildren I'll probably try to listen to their dreadful music. No-one likes a whiner … You, you're not a whiner either, I shouldn't say. Not as far as I know. If you whine I don't know who you do it to." They passed a brick wall covered in spray-painted faces, large and caricatured, with florescent pink skin. The sun glared through the windscreen; Pepper flipped down the shade. "You know what, Roan? I'm taking you to a place which is rather personal for me. A certain kind of personal, not picnic territory. I haven't even told Ms Limms. Don't worry it's nothing too sinister. We're nearly there. In fact … hup … yep, there." A long line of warehouses gave way in the distance to grass and dust and a dot of something else on the horizon. They drove quietly as it took shape, tall and boxy with grey brickwork and empty window frames. It marked the edge of the city; beyond it was wasteland.

"What is it?"

"My temple of doom, aha." Pepper parked the car, trotted ahead and made a sweeping gesture to the three storeys above him. Roan looked up as the wind lulled and it seemed the building held its breath.

"What do you think?" Pepper asked.

"What is this?"

"People all over the city know this place. Look at its big ugly face. You've heard me mention my wife, or have you? No perhaps you haven't. Did I ever tell you what happened to her?"

"No, you never mentioned her," Roan replied, wondering why he had never asked.

"Well I was married briefly. My wife left us. Horrible business. Her skin changed, she had fevers, hallucinated … Believed she was suffocating in snow."

"I'm sorry."

"Aha. That's the right thing to say. You're not normally good at that." He slapped Roan's shoulder, digging his fingers in. "This was the hospital. Or the building at least, you won't find much inside. It was due to be demolished. That was a while ago now. It was left to dilapidate, got overgrown, filled with wildlife, mostly human. They had tiptoe parties, sound systems to shake the ants out of the ground, thousands of people at once. They still do, I believe."

The two men entered through the space that was once a doorway. Their footsteps clomped along the floorboards. Roan peered into each room, half remembering something. The afternoon was still blazing outside and sunrays flooded through the gaps.

"Would you believe I own this building?" Pepper asked.

"I believe it if you tell me."

"Well I don't, aha … It keeps sucking me back though. Maybe it owns me."

"So who does own it?"

"The insects, I should say."

Roan noticed the scurrying around their feet. "Did you ever marry again?"

"No."

They were approaching the heart of the building, where light was scarce. Roan paced around restlessly, still with a memory he could not quite grasp. After a few more steps he clapped, suddenly invigorated. "Clement!"

Pepper turned to him. "Who might Clement be?"

"Oh sorry, I just remembered…" Pepper waited encouragingly. "We made up this silly kind of ghost story when we were first dating. It had a ghost," Roan snorted, "called Clement."

"Bit of a posh ghost was he?"

"Yea, he was a butler ghost and he haunted people by bringing them tea when they didn't want it."

"Scary fellow."

"Yea. That's been in my mind all day; I couldn't remember his name, and it was driving me nuts."

"And what happened to Clement?"

"Oh, we hoovered him."

"Ah." Pepper stroked his knuckles slowly across the wall. "You remind me so much of myself, it's astonishing."

"Did you and your wife make up a ghost story?"

He chuckled and shook his head slowly.

On their way home Roan's smirk remained. He was less attentive to the passing scenery and sat glazed over, humming so low that only he could hear.

"Well then. Here you are."

"Already?… Thanks, I suppose I'll see you in a while."

"I'll be by your spot again soon."

Roan clambered out. His smirk was all gone and he wished he could stay longer, but before he could think what to say Pepper drove off with a cheery beep.

"Damn it!" His voice sounded strange, like it was borrowed. The afternoon was growing cool and cloudy; he wondered what he ought to do for the rest of the day. As he fumbled for his keys he hummed some more, listening to the hollow sound, trying to imagine he could step back and study it like a museum exhibit. "Damn it!" He said it with more vigour this time as he walked up the stairs. As soon as he got into his flat he collapsed on the bed, staring vacantly upwards. "Idiot …" He put his hand in front of his mouth and repeated, feeling the vibrations of the word. "Iiidiiiiot."

He guessed it was five o'clock and turning he saw he was exactly right. Tomorrow was Sunday, a day off. Thirty-eight hours until he had to wake up for work again. After a minute or two of lying still, he began to pretend that he couldn't move, that he was paralysed or trapped under a spell. He thought about trying to move his foot, feeling it stuck in position, packed into place by the stodgy air. Perhaps he *was* trapped. Until his mind chose to move it, his body would be still. What if he never made that decision but sank further into idleness, until there was no way back? A fly buzzed onto his ear. He twitched, gave up the experiment and went to the bathroom.

As he turned on the light he caught his reflection in the mirror and stuck out his tongue. He saw his same face as it had been, late at night with her stray hairs clinging to it. He clasped the space where her torso had been, bent over the sink, rocking her body into him. The reflection stared back at him now, emotionless and intense; he forced an impish smile, then let it fall away. Still stroking the empty air, he stood there letting his mind settle, imagining with enough strength to momentarily touch her sweaty skin. Eyes still fixed on his reflection, he unbuttoned his jeans slowly, teasing as she had done. She moaned softly, meeting his gaze in the mirror. Roan rested one hand on the sink edge, just above hers, noticing each time she tightened her grip. His other hand was clasped as he rolled back and forth into it, listening to the soft slapping of his pelvis against her.

3

Ravers

"MILO!"

"What?"

"MILO! Put me on your shoulders, I want to touch the lasers."

"You're too fat. Let me get on *your* shoulders."

"I have to touch the lasers. Look at them!"

"I know they're …"

"MILO! Look at them, tell me you don't want to touch them!"

"I do. Let me get on your shoulders."

"Ok."

Milo clambered aboard. Once raised up he swayed his head from side to side, sticking his tongue out at the mass of people below. The vibrations of the music tickled his nose and made it itch. The ceiling dripped with evaporated sweat. He tried to reach the lasers but they moved higher, so he just closed his eyes and howled, his vocal cords rasping.

"This music is making me hot," he called down.

"What?"

"PASS ME THE WATER!"

"Sure!"

He took a couple of gulps, and passed it back. The lasers were lowering gradually; he stretched his arms up, noticing a girl some distance away doing the same from another set of shoulders. He waved at her but she was too engrossed to notice. Below him hot bodies danced against his legs. The bass faded out of the music, leaving a hum and a tick-tock. More arms were raised from all around, hooting, someone blew a whistle. Milo ran his fingertips through the lasers, cutting shadows in the green just as the beat dropped in and movement erupted again. He was lowered abruptly and his feet hit the ground.

"Milo!"

"What?"

"THIS DJ. HE'S LIKE … MY GUARDIAN ANGEL!"

Milo wiped the spray from his cheek. "You're spitting everywhere! And he's mine too."

"HE'S EVERYONE'S!" Aaron swung his arms out in a circle, catching a man next to them on the jaw. "Sorry! SORRY! Hit me back! Actually don't." A girl stumbled into them and turned to mouth an apology. Milo clasped her hand and spun her around. She smiled and nuzzled into him, then broke away into the crowd.

"Milo!"

"YEA?"

"I feel like this place is going to suck me back forever, until I'm one of those mashed-up old men in the rave who can't speak properly."

"Sounds like a plan."

"OOH MY GOSH THIS TUUUUUNE!"

"Aaron?"

"Milo, shush for a minute … Listen to this tune. Listen to this tune. Seriously." He had his arm clinched around Milo's neck. The two listened; there were words mixed in just below the beats. The air was thick with moisture. Aaron tilted his head back and yelled upwards then continued in Milo's ear. "Listen. It sounds like its saying *cough-drops*. Listen … *cough-drops* … *cough-drops* … *cough-drops*."

"It sounds like *locked-up*."

"Wait … *rock-salt*. It's *rock salt*."

"Pass the water please!" Milo took another swing, winking as he handed it back.

"You wink like a granddad."

"That's the best way to wink!"

"I invented a new dance today at work, but I forgot it."

"Shit. No."

A surge of people tipped them off balance. Milo ducked and slid between groups until he had his own section of dance floor again. Aaron had gone. A figure walked past, catching his eyes briefly.

"Tip-toe-tip-toe-tip-toe-tip … ?" The man's voice chimed into the beat. Milo searched his pockets until he felt a small plastic bottle; this was enough for the night. He shook his head at the man who passed on without acknowledgement. "Tip-toe-tip-toe-tip-toe-tip-toe?"

The crowd was closing in again. The heat made him dizzy, so he wrestled his way to the nearest wall and slumped down with his back against it. For some time he sat alone, bobbing involuntarily. The wall sent vibrations up his spine.

There was a thud. A large man with a shaggy beard sat at his side. Milo tried to speak but the music flooded into his mouth extinguishing the words. The man nodded knowingly then lifted his hands and began clapping. Milo joined. The man leaned in close enough to be heard. "I am a drummer. Here, do this…" He continued to clap as he had been doing, Milo followed. "No. No. Like this. *One two three four-one two-one two-one two three four.* Now you go… No. No. *One two*—not *one two three four-one two three four … two three four-one two-one two-one two three four.*"

For all he tried, Milo could not master it. Eventually the man shrugged and went on his way leaving him alone to dance with the top half of his body while his legs rested. He went to check the time on his phone, but reconsidered. Instead he rummaged back into his pockets and found something far more valuable. Knees disguising, he unscrewed the top and poured a few more drops onto his tongue. The bitterness spread through his whole mouth. He reached for the water; it wasn't there. With his face screwed up he clambered to his feet, scanning the room for Aaron amid the distortion of lasers.

"Can I have some of your water please? I'm dying." The woman obliged. "Thanks, oh my God." He was about to speak again when the beat of the music changed and he flung himself into the crowd. How could music do this to him? What was wrong with him? A doubt crept across his mind, a dread and he knew what it was. Postponing the inevitable he stood still, then finally reached for his phone to check the time. Just over two hours until he had to be at work.

The exhaustion that had been numbed for so long started to seep into him. A squat and pale skinned man was dancing nearby. Milo nodded a greeting. "I've got work in two hours." The man looked back at him absently. "I'VE GOT WORK IN TWO HOURS!"

"AHH! Too bad."

"Yea."

"That's not for two hours though."

"Yea, two hours."

"You tiptoed?" the man asked.

"Yea."

"What do you do?"

"I work in a call centre."

"Too bad, man. I hope you survive."

"What about you?"

The man wrapped his arm around the neck of the woman next to him. "We are going to disappear together."

"Disappear where?"

"I'm a romantic. He doesn't approve, does he Baby?" He turned and pressed his forehead into hers, pouting at the air. "She's my Baby." He kissed her. "Her name is Baby but I would call her it regardless. And I am Isa." He offered his hand.

"I know you, Isa … and Baby. I meet you here all the time!"

"… MILO! I'm so sorry," yelled Isa, embracing him with his free arm. "I'm so tiptoed, I barely know who I am, never mind you."

Milo chatted next to them, until they became engrossed in each other again. As he moved on, he took the vial from his pocket and swirled the liquid inside. If he didn't see Aaron in the next five minutes, then he would finish it. He bobbed around for a while, still gripping the container. When had the five minutes started, he wondered as he unscrewed the cap and swallowed the rest. Once again he had forgotten to find water first. Swearing to himself he moved through swarms of people, bumping into Aaron.

"MIIIIIIIIIIILOOOOOOOO!"

"AH! I missed you!"

"I missed you too."

"I need some water … Ah, thank you, that was so disgusting."

"We've got work soon."

"I was just thinking that."

"Do you have any left? I want to get destroyed while I still can."

"Oh shit! I finished it."

"Are you serious?"

"Sorry. I thought I wouldn't see you till the end."

"Milo …"

"I'm sorry. Really. We can buy some more."

"It doesn't matter. I shouldn't anyway."

"No, I'll buy you some more. I saw a guy earlier."

"It doesn't matter … Milo, you're a fucking donkey!"

"I know."

"You have to get high for both of us now. I'm gonna live through you."

"I will."

Within twenty minutes it took hold. Milo was blind to everything but colour and sound, unsure where the floor ended and his feet began. Faces flashed and faded around him, while he floated aimlessly like a ghost lost in smoke. Every once in a while he thrashed into dance, unable to focus his eyes. The lasers above were a blur of moving green. If somebody brushed against him he cast a smile vaguely in their direction, unsure if it would reach them.

Someone tugged on his arm. He turned and after a moment realised what was happening.

"NOOOO!"

"We have to. We start in half an hour."

4

Are you ill?

MILO SAT WITH HIS HEAD RESTING on one outstretched arm, viewing everything sideways. Rows of fingers on keyboards typing forwards instead of downwards. A dismal feeling gripped him. On the way to work he had tried to eat a sandwich and only progressed by five bites. Calls were being directed to him every three or four minutes, leaving time to resent the chattering around him and the chills from the air conditioner. No-one on his table had made any sales.

"I told 'im everything. Did the whole spiel. And he still wants to talk to his bloody wife first! No, you bastard, you buy it now or you bugger off!"

"Did you say that to him?"

"No, I should've bloody well said it to him. Listen to me, you cock sucker, you buy it now and get the free installation or I'll come to your house and install it myself. Up your fucking arse."

"Do you have experience with that type of installation, Jeff?"

"Yes very funny, in fact … *Well Good Morning. My name's Jeffrey. I'm calling from the* … Another one! Cunt!"

"I like it when you swear. It excites me."

"Well, if swearing's a crime, then you can fuck me in the, *Hi there …*"

"*Good morning my name's Aaron. I'm calling from* Thompson Optical. *Could I speak to Mr Rains please?*"

Milo's headset bleeped in his ear.

"*Hello, my name's Milo. I'm calling from* Thompson Optical. *Could I speak to Mrs Ellabeck please?*" An elderly woman grumbled something.

"*Mrs Ellabeck, how are you today?*"

"I don't want any holidays!"

"*I'm calling you because you recently expressed interest in our laser eye treatment.*"

"Who are you?"

"My name's Milo, I'm calling from …"

"Michaels?"

"… Thompson Optical. You filled in your details on our website. I'm calling to let you know you can book a free consultation …"

"I don't want any holidays. Or insurance. Or any of your gismos!"

"I'm …" She hung up.

Milo filled in the outcome menu on his screen – *Call back customer … in 20 minutes* – and lay back down. This day wasn't so bad; he had fought through worse before. When he arrived that morning he had gone straight to the toilet mirror to inspect his pupils. They weren't right. His skin was pasty and his t-shirt was smeared with stains that could have been blood. When he went into a cubicle to urinate he had a vague sensation of crowds watching him. Low level hallucinations. Walking to work, he had stared at each passing stranger in the street, sure it was someone he knew. "That's Janice, look it's Janice, oh no its not …" Aaron showed no interest. "Is that Callum? Aaron, its Callum. Oh … it's not." The only one he recognised correctly was the knight.

Waiting for calls was a rare luxury; often they piled through one after the other. Today he could doze between each beep – like a whole day of pressing the snooze button.

"Hi there, my name's Jeffrey, I'm calling from Norson Digitech. Am I speaking to a Mr Waterage? Hi there, I understand you recently expressed an interest in our state of the art digital television service. Television. That's right … Yes, I'm … Yes … Well that's brilliant, what sort of programs do you tend to watch? Well if we book it now we'll be able to enter you into … Ok. I see. No that's fine. Have a good day, Mr Waterage. Bye-bye now. This is just a fucking joke …"

The room was filled with rows of desks, banked together and facing each other in groups. Nearly two hundred people, all their voices mixed into one babbling wave. Some sat up-right examining computer screens, others lounged back in their chairs, a few paced around gesticulating into their ear pieces. Someone went to mark up a sale next to his name on the whiteboard. There was a faint ripple of applause. A pleasant anonymity kept Milo hidden amongst many other half-asleep workers. He thought about this with a smile as he sank deeper into his bicep, starting to cut off the blood. He enjoyed pins and needles, especially the first rush of cold as the numbness dispelled.

A few hours later he was ready to weep. The sun from outside dazzled him. The blind was broken and there was nowhere to move. People all around him grumbled about customers and hang-ups and narrowly missed sales. He lay there tensing every muscle in his face, trying to squeeze the world out of his ears. Before long he was weak and feared he would actually shed tears if he didn't get out of this mood. It was nearly lunchtime and there was a long day ahead.

"My name's Milo. I'm calling from Thompson Optical. *Could I speak to Mr Ruben please?"* His voice was deflated.

"There's no Mr Ruben here. There is a Mr Roburn. What might this be concerning?"

"Mr Roburn … expressed interest in our laser eye treatment … Could I speak to him?"

"I am he."

To relieve his boredom Milo tried something: *"EXCELLENT! HOW ARE YOU TODAY MR ROBURN, BUDDY?"* Jeff flinched at the sudden change. The people opposite glanced up in vague amusement.

"… Busy."

"WELL THAT'S SMASHING, THAT IS!"

"What can I do for you?"

"NOT WHAT YOU CAN DO FOR ME, IT'S WHAT I CAN DO FOR YOU, MR ROBURN, BUDDY!"

"Must you speak at that volume?"

"I'm going to book you in for the CONSULTATION OF A LIFETIME!"

Mr Roburn hung up.

He sat up straight and stretched his arms out. A girl dressed in black leggings and a lacy blue shirt wafted past, her perfume sent a burst of adrenaline through him. He yanked himself free from the headset and strode around to where Aaron was sitting.

"Milo, I got a sale. In this condition. I'm such a trooper."

"Go and put it on the board."

"Fuck the board."

"Don't you want a round of applause?"

"Where are you going for lunch?"

"AARON GOT A SALE! OH YES HE DID! WE LOVE YOU AARON! YEAH! GO AARON!" Milo clapped emphatically, until the applause spread through the room. Aaron blushed slightly and raised his fist at Milo's grinning face.

"Where are you going for lunch?" he repeated.

"I don't want to eat anything. I want to down a glass of cheap disgusting whisky."

"Seriously?"

"Don't be like that, come have a drink."

"Milo … do you know how sick I feel?"

"What are you going to do instead?"

"You're a nasty man."

"What are you going to do?"

"I'm going to sit next to a tramp and talk to him about the trials of life."

"Ha, that's what I thought."

"Enjoy your disgusting lunch."

Milo moved around the room asking more people. It was not uncommon to take a liquid lunch in his profession, but on this day nobody had the stomach to join.

"Beth, come with me to the Stag and get slightly wasted."

"Wow that sounds lovely. I've eaten already though."

"So?"

"Not today mate."

"Fuck! What's wrong with this company?"

He asked another seven people, getting more animated each time, using all the sales technique he had been sleeping on all morning. At last he gave up, buzzed himself out and headed to the pub alone. As he walked each person and thing seemed uncomfortably close to him. He shuddered, resisting the urge to shove people out of his way. When he arrived he slapped the bar with both his hands.

"Whisky … please." He slugged the contents of the glass, groaning and scrunching his mouth in a happy grimace. After ordering a second to sip, he swivelled around on a stool to face the room. Three men with suitcases sat together eating pies and arguing. A few other figures hunched alone over their pints. Above them, along the wall, black and white film stars beamed at Milo from their frames. It was dim despite the sunshine outside. His phone buzzed; he hadn't looked at it all day and there were four unread messages:

Aaron: *DUUUUUUDE WHERE ARE YOU?????*

Erin: *You were at The Hospital and u didn't invite me?? Gayboy! X*

Jade: *Ur a twisted fuck! Xx.*

Ivy: *You're not coming home tonight then … ?*

Milo took a sip, concentrating, trying to work out the brand.

"You!" He looked around and saw a woman standing by him. It was Nadine, a colleague who sat next to him occasionally. She liked to flirt over the phone and cackle at her own jokes. Milo had never warmed to her. "Hi," he replied.

"Drowning our sorrows, are we?"

"Yea."

"What happened? You can tell me."

He was bemused for a moment. "Nothing."

"Here you are, all alone. Tell me what happened." She edged towards him with a mothering look.

"I wanted to taste whisky. Because it's sour and disgusting."

"U-huh?"

"Yea."

She sat by him, drawing her stool too close.

"I heard they do good soup here on Thursdays. I thought it was Thursday. How dumb am I?" He was about to reply but instead just continued to stare at her, wondering if she would get flustered. There were faint lines on her brow. How old was she again? After a time she struggled to fill the silence.

"You know my friend, yesterday right … Well not yesterday, but recently. This taxi driver kicked her, cos she didn't wanna pay the fare. She said it was too much and got out. Then he got out and kicked her leg and fractured it."

"Yea?"

"Isn't that horrible?"

"Yea."

"He should get arrested!"

"Are you buying soup?

"I can't, can I? It's not Thursday. You might have to buy me a drink."

"I was bad to a cab driver once."

"Really?"

"Yea."

"Ha! What did you do?" She was smiling at him. Still too close. Her features were slightly thick set, but she was pretty. Why did he find her so repulsive?

"Let's sit on that sofa."

"OK." She followed and they sat next to each other. Milo collapsed back and closed his eyes. He felt her tapping his knee.

"You're weird," she said.

"Yea." Milo swigged some more. The alcohol hit his ailing body with a surprising kick. His legs were warm with tipsy blood. She was leering at him expectantly. Maybe he ought to kiss her out of the blue. There was a peculiar irritation in him. He wanted to say something to wound her so she scampered away. Or perhaps he just wanted to manhandle her and gag her mouth. He touched her arm and was about to speak again but was cut off by a surge of nausea.

"Wait for me a second." He stumbled from the sofa straight to the toilet and was puking before he got to the bowl. Not much came out; he hadn't eaten for hours. When he finished he gargled some water and strolled back out.

"I just puked."

Nadine looked blankly at him. She seemed offended. At last she came out with "Eugh!"

Milo laughed so much his stomach ached and he felt like retching again. When it subsided he dropped into the sofa. The girl watched him nonplussed. Something akin to pity brewed in him.

"Are you ill?" she asked.

Milo considered the question. "No."

"You seem like one of these weird guys in a movie that are going to die in a week."

"I know. I like that."

5

Have a listen

THIS WAS PATCHY BUT STRONG. Roan thought it over through breakfast, alternating between sips of tea and tap water. It stayed on his mind throughout the day. He was back at work and expected to see Pepper again. Waiting for his arrival kept him on edge. The state of mind he needed was not quite accessible and this made the time drag slowly.

While at drama school he had briefly been a life drawing model. Somehow she had roped him into it. A room full of eyes on his naked body and nowhere to hide but inside himself. This was how he learnt to disappear. Roan spent the morning aching under the weight of his costume. His mentor arrived at noon.

"Hello, and don't worry. You don't have to talk to me. I'm on form today. So I won't be sitting here long. Just a couple of dozen wallets left. They'll all be gone by the evening." He sounded more hoarse than usual. *She's got your wallet!* Roan remembered it. She had kissed him by the train doors, just before they started closing and he jumped aboard. *She's got your wallet!* someone joked, making Roan smirk inanely.

Two men passed nearby. Pepper slapped his knee hard and stood up. "Gents good morning, would you like to melt a heart without having to get your cock out? Aha. Hello to both of you. I have what you need." The men listened without stopping and left without speaking. Pepper returned to his seat. "I'm still on form though; they were a warm up." Roan found that he was breathing cautiously, as though to avoid detection. "Well then. If you have nothing further to add, I'll be off. I'll pop back for a visit later."

Once Pepper had gone, Roan tried to sink into his familiar trance but it still eluded him. His legs grew heavy and the heat of the sun-baked metal made him queasy. The more the discomfort grew the more he concentrated on it, imagining it was a new pleasure that his body craved. His feet were melting into the pedestal and his lips were salty. At last stillness folded cosily over him, his thoughts converged from chaos into a slow procession moving in front of him one by one, mixed in with the passing people.

Years ago he'd had recurring dreams: beetles everywhere. Not crawling up his legs, just crunching underfoot. Those dreams had sickened him but they only lasted a few days. What had caused them? The next thought passed before him and he remembered the day. She had stung her leg on a nettle. He was clambering for dock leaves when he noticed them, hundreds of them. They squeezed flat underfoot and he shivered but said nothing. Later on she said something that had made him laugh; he had wondered if it was actually funny, or did love make him prone to over-smiling?

Humour had become a peculiar thing to him. In recent months he had watched the world ever more intently, searching for it. The scarcity did not surprise him, although it filled him with a slight melancholy, the kind that comforts more than it disturbs. His thinking continued in this way, one thought at a time and no more. What luxuries he kept secret in his metal body. None of these people walking past really knew his name or story; this dawned on him and it brought such relief he almost laughed. Was that humour? Each time he had laughed came back to him now in turn; he scrutinised each one.

The surroundings had changed. The sun was now warming a different side of him. He must have been gone for three hours, maybe more. As he fully came to, Roan became aware of a voice beneath him.

"…of course I'd never seen snow at that age. Who has these days?" It was Pepper. He was sitting somewhere by his feet, just out of sight. How long had he been there? "I've found a way to make it now. It's one of my stranger tricks." It was getting late in the evening he guessed by the amount of people coming out the buildings. "I suspect you're awake by now, Mr Knight. I've been observing and I suspect it's around this time." A hand thudded lightly on his leg plate. "I've been talking to a coma patient, haven't I?" Roan's toes shifted around inside his shoes, he cleared his throat. "I bowled them over. What about you? Did you bowl them over today…? I'll tell you what." He stood up and faced Roan. "While I'm here… let me show you a trick. You know, magic is gradual like a volume knob." Out of his pocket he took a black handkerchief and held it out by the top corners. "So… have a listen." With a swift movement he pulled the corners outward, stretching the fabric till it cascaded out from itself, spreading with his hands into the size of a bed sheet. Roan lurched at the sudden flood of blackness. All around was dark, but for the streetlights glinting in the puddles. Rain tinkled onto his head and shoulders. It was way past the end of his day; he stepped down carefully from his pedestal and flexed both his legs.

"Good night Mr Knight. Aha!"

6

Monsters

IVY DREW THE CURTAINS OPEN and leapt backwards in shock. The light revealed her husband huddled on the sofa, gaping at her wide-eyed. On the adjacent sofa sat Aaron. Both were wrapped in blankets and deathly pale.

"Good morning," Milo croaked at her. She gave an unconvincing laugh and traipsed over to open the other curtains. "I didn't want to wake you. So I stayed down here."

"Thanks." The garden outside was wild with neglect, honing in towards her day by day. "Where did you go?"

"I've been to some … I don't even know what it was. Some crazy place." His pupils were large with only a sliver of blue around them. His mouth was twisted slightly, perhaps he was smiling.

"Lucky you're off today," she replied at last. He nodded.

"Call in sick. You can stay with us." The invitation came from Aaron, who peeked at her from under his quilt, with the same peculiar twisted lip.

"No thanks."

Milo made a noise that began as a laugh and trailed off in laziness. She left them and went back into the kitchen to make breakfast.

The fridge was crammed with milk and loaves of bread that hadn't been there the night before. She made herself some toast and coffee and sat down at the table. Someone shouted to her. With a pang of irritation she went back through.

"What is it, I can't hear you?"

"Do you have any oranges, Ivy?" It was Aaron, his head hanging over the arm of the sofa.

"We've got orange juice."

"No, it needs to be oranges. The fruit." She turned to go back. "How are you, Ivy?"

"Ok. Busy."

"Yea, teachers. You're busy. You teachers."

"We are."

"Too much teaching, that's the problem." He flopped back in a silent laugh. Milo joined in from the other side of the room.

"I'm going to have some breakfast," she sighed.

"Bring your breakfast through here."

"I don't eat in here. It keeps the mice out."

"We already have mice," said Milo.

"What?"

"Or a mouse. Just one. Or maybe a bug … I didn't really see."

"We have mice?" She scanned the floors.

"Maybe."

"Are you sure?"

"I saw it the other night. But it was quick … so I'm not sure what it was." His voice was monotonous, even more so than usual. Ivy turned, clicking the door behind her. Her throat was tight. The toast popped up and she crunched it dutifully though her appetite was gone.

"And why did Colin run away from the monster?"

"COS IT WAS A MONSTER!"

"Right. And why would he run away from a monster?"

"Cos it's scary and it might eat him."

"But the monster didn't want to eat Colin, did it? What did the monster want? Anyone else?" The same boy had given her the last three answers, Ivy scanned the room. A girl with wiry ginger hair piped up from the back.

"He wanted to take Colin to the monsters' party."

"It did. And why do you think the monster wanted to do that, Kirsty?"

The girl pondered.

"He's … I don't know." She blushed and waited for Ivy to move on. The class turned to her. "… I think the monster didn't think he was a monster."

"Oooo I see. Why do you think that?"

"He was a nice monster, he just looked funny and had big teeth, but he only ate leaves with them."

"Interesting. I like it."

All thirty children sat cross legged in front of her, a few peering up, others murmuring. Two boys at the back were tearing up bits of carpet and throwing them around. "OK EVERYONE BACK TO YOUR SEATS!" A noise of disapproval erupted. Ivy wrote the word *MONSTER* on the board and waited as they found their way back.

"Soooo … monsters. What do you think it means to be a monster? Any ideas?" No one volunteered. "Imagine we built our own monster, how would it look?"

"Big teeth!"

"Claws!"

"BIG FACE!"

"One at a time! Put your hands up." A dozen hands shot up. A few of them shook frantically. Ivy looked for somebody who hadn't yet spoken.

"Jason?"

"Can we give him bad breath?"

"Of course!" She turned and started a list. "Jenny?"

"He's got really big claws."

"I SAID BIG CLAWS BEFORE!"

"Calm down Howard. Hand up next time. Who else? Richie?"

"BIG FACE!"

"Ok, thanks for putting your hand up this time. So we've got big claws and a big face and bad breath. Caitlin, what do you think we should give him … or it?"

"Big legs and arms."

"Ok, let's just put *big*, shall we? That can go nicely with what we've said already."

"BIG BOOBS!"

"Calm down Howard! Now what else apart from big? What shall we give our monster? Danny?"

"What about a gun?"

"You think the monster should have a gun?"

"Yea, one of the ones that shoots out a million bullets every second."

"Ok, let's give him a gun."

"YOU CAN'T HAVE A MILLION BULLETS A SECOND. THAT'S STUPID. MY DAD'S IN THE ARMY." Ivy glared towards the outburst. "Sorry, Miss."

Who'd been waiting the longest? Many looked pained from holding up their hands.

"Cassie?"

"Miss, I think the monster should have bad thoughts," she said smugly.

"That *is* interesting. What do you mean by that, Cassie?"

"He thinks about bad things."

"Cassie, you're a star … Ok, this is enough to get on with. What we're going to do now … you're all going to design your own monsters. Use some of the ideas we've had up here if you need to. Draw *and* label. And make them as crazy as you can – really bring them to life. If you need help, hand up. If not, get going." The scribbling began.

It wasn't long until lunch. Her stomach was tight with hunger; every now and again it rumbled loudly, making the kids nearest her gawp curiously. She strolled and inspected work, making *ums* of approval every now and again.

"MISS! Miss, Hector's crying!" At the end of the room sitting with his back to her, Hector was hunched over, twitching.

She hurried over. "Hector, what's wrong?" He whimpered and sucked in a snotty breath. "Shall we go outside and talk about it?" After a few more sobs he nodded. Halfway out she realised she couldn't leave the other children alone, so they went to a far corner. She knelt down in front of him. "Why are you crying?" The classroom chatter rapidly turned to chaos, people stood up to see them and bickered over personal space. She tried to give them an icy look, but only a few noticed. "EVERYBODY SIT DOWN!" It took a few seconds for them to react. Long enough to wonder what she would do if they ignored her.

Hector tried to speak. "I don't …" He shook his head firmly. "I don't like monsters."

"Honey, they're not real. We're just drawing some silly pictures."

"But you said … they're going to come to life!"

"Oh for heaven's sake … I meant we should draw them nicely."

"But you said they'd come to life. I hate monsters."

"I wanted us to bring them to life … That was just my way of saying I wanted us to draw them well. It's a way adults talk sometimes."

"Carne said that because you said …"

"What did Carne say?"

"MY MONSTER'S FAT AND BALD AND HE'S HECTOR'S DAD!"

"Whoever said that, you're in big trouble! What did Carne say to you?"

"Nothing."

"All we're doing is drawing some pictures. It's fun. Then we're going to put them on the display board, the one that's been empty and it's going to make the classroom look a lot better. That's all."

"Then why did you say we're going to bring them to life?" He tried to swallow back his tears as embarrassment set in.

"Hector …" She sighed. "Remember how I told everyone that my sister and I had painted this room yellow in the holidays before the start of this year? Well we painted it to bring the room to life. That doesn't mean the room actually comes alive, it just means we painted the walls and now it's livelier and a more fun place to be." Hector wiped his nose on his sleeve. "They're just pictures, they can't hurt you … Now, are you ready to draw a picture for me?" He nodded without looking up. "Off you go."

Just a few minutes were left. The sun glared through, making the walls glow. She regretted choosing such a garish yellow.

"The bell's going to ring in a couple of minutes and I want … Errrm no! In a couple of minutes, not now. Hand in your papers to my desk when you leave. And I want Carne to stay behind and talk to me." Carne watched her from the back of the room with his pencil wrapped up in one fist and a blank sheet of paper in front of him.

"Did you need to do that?"

"What?"

"You upset Hector. He told me you …"

"Hector upset himself."

"Carne, I'm not trying to tell you off …"

"HA! HA!" Both his elbows leaned together on the desk, his palms pressed against his temples.

"Why did you do it?" He locked his sunken eyes onto her and bit his nail. His shoulders and back curled forwards as if someone had bent him out of shape. "We have this talk a lot don't we Carne …? Are you going to talk to me today …?" He inspected the nail he'd been biting then looked back at Ivy. "What can I do to make things better for you?"

"I don't want things to get better."

"That's a funny thing to say." He rubbed his cheeks and yawned. "Are you happy here?"

"Here and now, with you?"

"In my class."

"I don't need to learn how to draw monsters."

"Is the work too easy for you?"

"Or times tables, or about the planets and stars and everything else."

"It's not about the facts, it's about learning to think like a grown up."

"I'm not going to be a grown up."

"You're going to be Peter Pan?"

"HA!"

"I didn't want to grow up when I was your age either."

"I said I won't, not I didn't want to."

Ivy pulled her chair in closer. "You're a clever one, Carne."

"You're a boring one."

"But you need to learn to speak properly to people. Especially when they're trying to help you."

"Everyone's trying to help me."

"You say it like it's a bad thing."

"People talking all calm and smooth like panda bears."

"Let me tell you a secret," she said after a moment's thought.

"When I was a girl I hated school."

"Really?" He was unenthused.

"When I was your age, if someone told me I was going to be a teacher, I would have laughed a big rude laugh like yours – HA! HA! HA!"

"You keep pretending you're like me."

"I'm just telling you a story …"

"No-one's like me."

"I know it must be hard for you being different."

"I don't care."

"What do you care about?" She scanned him for clues. Nothing showed, but a scowl too jaded for a child. He slithered down his seat, drawing his heels around in circles on the floor. His trousers were worn through at the knees, revealing the callused flesh beneath. "Go and get your lunch, we'll talk another time." He lowered himself to the floor and slunk away on his hands and knees. "Do you need me to get the door?" He reached up to pull the handle before she caught up. In the corridor a group of children made way as he approached. He crawled between them and round the corner out of sight.

7

An empty morning

MILO WOKE EARLY WITH A START. The house was empty. He went straight to the shower, turned the dial to cold and savoured the shock. After breakfast, in an effort to amuse himself, he called through nearly twenty people in his phone but it was too early and nobody picked up. So instead, he meticulously shaved the hairs out of his nose, exploring the crevices of each nostril. It was strangely engrossing. This done, he wandered naked around the house and turned on the TV. A man with a microphone smiled till his gums showed. He turned it off again. The same angst from the other day was back, festering in his abdomen. Too much energy and nothing to do. He shadowboxed around the living room until he was wheezing and then sat on the carpet, wondering who might be watching from the houses across the street. Taken by the idea, he stood up again and pointed accusingly out the window.

After putting some shorts on, he killed more time doing press ups and running up and down the stairs. At last he settled, listening to the traffic outside. Today he was going to call Nadine he had decided somewhere in the press ups. At work they had talked of meeting and having soup. He had thrown out the invitation more from habit than desire; since then her number had lain dormant in his phone, waiting to be used at some empty time like this.

Ivy would be home in the evening; his guest needed to be out and the room aired before then. He pressed the call button, plugged the headset into the phone and lay back on his bed. The rings continued until he was about to give up, then a feeble "Hello". He had woken her.

"Hey."

"Milo?"

"Hey, I'm going to the shops. Come with me."

"What's … What for?"

"For shopping."

"You woke me up for this?"

"I woke you up..?"

"Yes."

"Yes …"

"Milo, seriously. It's too early. What do you want?"

"To go shopping."

"Now?"

"Are you awake?"

"I am now."

"Me too …"

"You're such a weirdo."

"Where do you live?" Milo picked up the phone from his chest, balancing it on three fingers, then two, then one.

"Where do you want to go?" she asked.

"I haven't decided yet. Text me your address. I'll pick you up."

"Can't we meet this evening?"

"No, it needs to be now."

"Ok … This better be the best shopping I've ever had."

"See you in an hour."

"Make it two."

"Ok, bye."

A young mousy woman in a dressing gown opened the door and led him in. Milo followed, wondering at her dark hair all ruffled up at the back. Maybe she was just a rough sleeper? They came to a small living room with faux leather sofas and movie posters spread unevenly over the walls. One side of the room was stacked high with books and DVDs. Clothes and other debris littered the floor, tangled together with unravelled masking tape and electrical cables. A hookah pipe between the two sofas leant precariously to one side, surrounded by dots of ash and burns on the carpet. Two men in their twenties sat cross legged in front of the TV playing computer games, filling the room with gunshot sounds. The girl walked into the adjoining kitchen and out of sight. Partially separating the rooms was a large black worktop with a built-in fish tank. Milo sat down.

"You wanna sign the table?" one of the gamers enquired without looking back. Milo studied the table in front of him. It was covered in scratched writing and burns or black stains shaped like a woman's breasts.

"Sure." He fished through his pockets for a key. "How did you burn that picture on?"

"Blow torch and tangerine skin."

"Ok."

"You cut the skin into a stencil, then burn around. You like it?"

"Yea, it's … You've still got the blow torch?"

"Yea, it's down the side of the sofa. Do one if you want." Milo rooted around until he felt a metal handle. "I'm not sure if there's gas in it though. Hey, you're Milo, the dude with a wife?"

"Yea."

"I'm Brendan."

Milo twisted the nozzle until the gas hissed and the flame blared into life. "Are you students?" He adjusted between yellow and blue flames, flicking a finger through each.

"I am, she's not. Nadine's not, obviously."

"Yea? What about you?" The friend was too absorbed to reply.

"He's a student too. He doesn't live here though."

"What can I use as a stencil?"

"Anything that won't catch fire."

He took two copper coins out of his pocket and placed them next to each other on the table, running the flame over them till the surrounding wood was dark brown. When he was done, without thinking, he picked one up again.

"FUCK!"

Brendan looked back, and laughed. "Rookie mistake!"

Small blisters were forming on the ends of his finger and thumb. Milo chuckled loudly, the flame still roaring in one hand. "Do your fish have names?" he brushed the coins along the table with the corner of a magazine to reveal perfect circles.

"They do, I can't remember them though. They're Amy's. We were going to name them after us but we thought if your one died you might think you were going to die too."

Under the sofa Milo found a small pencil, he lined it up on the table below the circles he had just made.

"Can I burn this pencil?"

"Alright."

Milo lowered the flame over it and waited. Finally he turned the torch off, set it aside and blew the blackened pencil back onto the floor revealing a tightly shut mouth below the two eyes. The face above the breasts frowned up at him, blank and incurious. Just then Amy came back into the room, eating a bowl of cereal, and sat on the other sofa.

"What are your fish call—?" He was interrupted by Nadine's entrance from the other door.

"OH MY GOD! How long have you been here?"

"Oh, I was supposed to tell you he had come," said Amy between crunches.

"I've been up in my room waiting like an idiot!"

"Yea, well he's here."

"Hi," Milo added benignly. She walked over to him, passing her hand over his hair and sitting down.

"It's weird to see you out of work Milo …"

"Really?"

"You look strange without a headset and microphone."

"Ha." Milo stared at the fish, trying to think of a comeback. In his pocket his phone vibrated. He went to retrieve it, then changed his mind.

For a while longer they sat and small-talked. Nadine pulled gently at the hairs on his arm. He wished he could blow her friends away like a nursery rhyme wolf. While she nattered in one ear, he pursed his lips ever so slightly and blew in the direction of the two boys. It didn't work, so he went for the next best thing. He headed for the door.

"Where are you going?" He gestured for her to follow, realising how clumsy this was: everyone knew what he was trying to do. She was embarrassed but reluctantly followed. Together they left the room. He led, sauntering as though he had no plan. She caught up to him and tried to speak but he got in first.

"I wasn't going to call you. I don't know why. Usually I don't think about things this much." She peered into him. "The thing is …" What else was she thinking? He examined her: she was softening, but still suspicious. "I feel suspicious of people sometimes. I want to trust them … This must sound stupid."

"I'm like that too." There was a rattle from a hamster cage on the floor. He made as if to speak, but let the breath slide out and touched his lips onto hers. Immediately she pressed into him hard, wrapping her arms around his neck. Her eyes were closed, his remained open a few seconds longer.

In his pocket the phone vibrated again, as if in protest at being squashed between their bodies. Nadine felt it too and parted from him momentarily. There was another noise. The hamster had climbed up the bars of its cage and hung there precariously.

"He's watching us," he muttered.

"It's a she."

"That's ok then."

Her kiss twisted into a smile. "No, it's not." She took him by the hand and led him to the stairs. Her bedroom door slammed shut behind them. He pressed her up against the wall, just as his phone vibrated again. He tilted his leg away, but it was too late.

"Who keeps calling you?"

"Who cares?"

"Is it your wife?"

"She's at work." Her lips slipped clumsily down his chin and back to his mouth. He pressed his thigh between her legs and explored the soft flesh above the belt of her jeans. Her legs squeezed in around him. In the few stumbling steps to the bed Milo undid her belt. She seemed uncertain and kissed him back rigidly, as he tugged her t-shirt up.

"Milo, we …" He smothered the words with his mouth and bit on her lip. She squeaked, and tried to speak again. He gave her his neck, unhooking his socks with either toe. Her arms were spread either side limply.

"Milo I can't …"

"Neither can I." He replied immediately kissing her again. For a few seconds she submitted, then suddenly levered herself from under him with surprising strength. "You've got a wife. Why are you doing this to her?"

"I know this is wrong…" It was all he could think of, so he lunged towards her again. She deflected him and stood up, jeans unbuttoned and hair tangled.

"Milo. What's your wife's name?"

He collapsed onto the bed. "If you're going to be like this… I'm going to sleep."

Nadine pulled her top back on and threw the socks from the floor to their owner.

"Ok." The window and curtains had been open the whole time and a soft wind brushed between his bare toes. When he had calmed down he sat back up. She was perched on the corner of the bed, hugging her knees and looking at him.

"Don't be angry with me," she said in a commanding tone.

"I'm not." He laughed and watched her tuck a strand of hair behind her ear, feeling like he knew her despite the little they had said.

"You married young."

"Yea." He reached for the duvet bunched up at the corner of the bed; she handed it to him. They remained this way for a very long time, Milo wrapped in her duvet, Nadine leaning against his legs.

"If you get another fish… will you name it after me? It's the least you can do."

"I'll tell Amy. I hate fish."

8

Sylvie

ALONG WITH THE SWARM, Milo emerged out onto the platform. It was busy with babbling and Friday night squeals. He darted through the gaps in the crowd, along the edge above the tracks. His body tensed up in case he was nudged. The rumble of the approaching train stirred the rabble further. He glanced down at the live rail as its charge rippled through and the announcement came. *I hope…* he thought, tiptoeing to pass another group. The train thundered out of the tunnel; he tensed up further, skipping along the edge… *I hope…* looking down at the darkness below the platform, wondering what it would be like. The train buffeted past, blocking the view and the strange thoughts. The doors opened and he slid into the last remaining seat, resting his legs for the long walk ahead.

"Say when."

"… When. When! Fucking when!"

"Haha!" Milo handed the cup to Aaron, who took a sip and tightened his cheeks in disgust. They waited in a hoard of people beneath the silhouette of the giant building. Green lasers darted from the window frames and out into the night. They were both feeble from all the walking. Milo's shoes were grey with dust and his skin clammy in the late summer air.

"How much do you have?" Aaron asked, looking at Milo's shoes where the vials of tiptoe were hidden.

"Plenty!"

Aaron took another sip. "How long do you think we'll be drinking from plastic cups?"

"I love plastic cups."

"They make me feel like a teenager."

Milo swirled his drink and sniffed it. "Next time I'll get brandy and some of those big round glasses." A gust of wind scattered dust over the crowds, Milo shielded his cup. More people seeped through the doorway, the two of them shuffled forward, closer to the thumping bass.

"When's everyone else getting here?" Milo asked.

"It's just us tonight."

"Again? Do we have any friends left?"

Aaron shrugged. They drew closer to the entrance. The drumbeat was clearer from here. Milo nodded, his heart whirling against his ribs in a sickening excitement. He tapped his toes. Aaron patted his spiked-up hair and wiped the sweat from his forehead. Two looming men guarded the doorway, folding and unfolding their arms in slow deliberation. A woman with a clipboard stood next to them, twiddling a pen.

Another wave of dust powdered over them. The music inside had slowed to a murmur, the bass gone for a moment, gathering up for the next drop. They edged forward a little more. Above them the building bore down, obscuring half the sky. People hooted from within as the music elevated back towards a drumbeat. The windows flickered with strobe light. The group ahead of them moved through the opening, revealing the woman with the clipboard tilted lazily. Milo took a step forward, scrutinizing her in disbelief. She waited coolly, sheltered from the wind by a doorman's torso. Milo hesitated, unsure whether or not to mention it.

"Seen a ghost?"

He muttered inaudibly and turned to see Aaron caught in similar puzzlement.

"Have you been here before?" she asked, faintly amused.

"Yes," grunted Milo, "… I have. We have. It keeps sucking me back."

"It does that. Full name?"

"Milo Blakely."

"Milo … And you?"

"Aaron Sapsted."

She slid her pen down the list and made two crosses. "In you go."

The music switched to a pitter-patter, with a low humming. Milo swayed and jiggled his feet.

"Keep still," barked the bouncer patting him down. They passed the threshold.

"Yaaaaaaaaa!" Milo screamed and skipped into the sea of green light and flailing limbs.

"Do you feel it yet?" Aaron yelled.

"I'm not sure. You?"

Aaron shook his head and shimmied. "Fat guys feel it last."

Milo closed his eyes, swirling his arms around the empty darkness. Over an hour ago they had emptied the first vial. Since then he had been waiting, aching to be under the spell again and second guessing every rush of warmth in his cheeks.

But then – something. A blanket of tingling. It wasn't imagined. The warmth moved though his body, soothing then escalating into a crippling wave of pleasure. Half opening his eyes, he saw Aaron bathed in green, stupefied in smiles. The crowds brushed against him. Milo sidestepped and felt his brain spinning as he did.

"I need to sit down."

Their ears hummed as they emerged into the fresh air. Milo led the way, a cigarette hanging unlit from his mouth. Out here people sat around in groups, lounging back on their elbows. He flicked the cigarette to life and collapsed onto the ground, head tilted back.

"I can't feel the smoke," he said to Aaron as he botched up a smoke ring. "But I can see it, so I know it's there."

"I know what you mean." Aaron clambered down next to him. "They feel like those plastic quitting sticks, whatever they're called."

"You know, if I ever get addicted to smoking it won't be for the nicotine, it'll be the feeling of blowing smoke at the sky."

Aaron followed suit, watching the patterns as they rose and listening to the buzz of mixed up voices. "Milo, don't you think it's crazy..." He stopped as though undecided what to mention first. "...that most people spend most of their time indoors?"

"Crazy."

"Indoors isn't even in the world, this is the world. When we were cave men, how much time do you think we spent in actual caves?"

"You love talking about cave men. I've noticed that about you."

"I love a lot of things. Don't get me started on loving things."

Milo swallowed hard as the next wave of tiptoe swam through him. "You love to love," he said when it passed.

"Milo … did you notice the woman on the door?"

"You saw that too? I thought I was imagining it."

"I saw it all right."

"I've been thinking about it ever since we got in."

Aaron shook his head reflectively, then laughed. "Fuck! My cigarette's finished already. How slowly are we talking?"

Milo looked at the stubs they were holding. "Yea. Everyone's out there living and getting things done and we're like – *hooooooooooow slooooooooowly weeeeeeeere weeeeeee* … Ha! Ha! Ha! Ha!"

They shifted to turn their backs to the wind and the dust. "I suppose it's not surprising," Aaron continued. "We must all have look-a-likes."

"It's true, there's probably hundreds of all of us."

"Yea. Imagine if all the people who looked like you went to the same place at the same time. That would be a mind fuck."

Milo drew a circle in the dust. "Ivy doesn't even know places like this exist," he said, thinking back to the woman on the door and the familiar redness of her lips.

"Imagine life without places like this."

"… Just work and home and getting older."

"They don't know how good things can be. Another ciggie?"

Milo accepted. "Wise words as usual."

"It's easy to sound wise here." Aaron gestured to the building towering above them. "You can say anything here and it will come out all profound."

"You think? Say something profound about … vomit."

"Ok. Let me think for a sec … A man … wait. A man who vomits will taste his food twice but still go hungry."

"Haha! That was awesome. You should be speaking from a mountaintop."

"Tomorrow I'll be me again."

"Enjoy it while it lasts, eh? You ready to go in?"

"I am, after one question."

"What's that?"

Aaron paused. "I've asked you before. But maybe because we're here you might answer … Where do you go when you do your little disappearing act?"

"I disappear. Haha!"

Aaron tutted. "I'm not going to stop asking you know."

"Be my guest."

"I'll find out one of these days … Let's go in."

"Time to dance yourself thin."

"… Time to dance yourself clever."

The ground was dappled with cigarette butts, half buried in the gathering dust.

"Back into the midst!" Aaron called from ahead.

"The mist?"

"That too."

The music and the heat hit them and made them swoon. The ceiling flashed. Somewhere in the blur Aaron vanished. As was their custom they continued separately, trying to remember everything to share when they met again. Maybe they could. The rush had steadied, leaving only a boundless energy and peace. Next to him was a lanky man in a camouflage hat. He nudged Milo, pointed to the speakers and grimaced in pleasure. Milo grimaced back.

It was too dark to know for sure, but Milo cut through the crowds until he was in the centre of everything. *It keeps sucking me back,* he had said. *It's magnetic.* Had she said that? What had she said? He turned to see her, blissfully dancing and unaware of him.

"Hey!" he shouted. "When I saw you at the door, you surprised me."

"I noticed."

"Don't you want to know why?"

She wavered to the music as though she hadn't heard him, and then said, "I know about you."

"Really?"

"Milo." Her dark red hair hung haphazardly across one side of her face. "The one with a wife."

"Ha!"

"Poor you."

"Poor me?"

"Poor Milo."

"I'm not poorly at the moment." He had to yell above a wobbling new bass line.

"No-one's poorly here."

"Who are you then?"

"Sylvie."

"Sylvie who?" The question was lost in the buzzing.

"I've not seen you here before, Milo."

"I came here once. I had to come back."

"It's magnetic."

"You seem like you belong here … like some dark, rave princess." He looked over her shoulder at the sweaty jungle that seemed to go on forever.

She followed his lead. "There're lots of people like me and like you."

"You think?"

"I meet them every time I come here."

"I like people like me," he said, talking to the slight dimple in her chin and the flush in her cheeks.

"You think you're special, Milo; you're not special to anyone."

"I don't need to be special."

She was dancing closer to him now, mouthing her words carefully as if he was reading her lips. "What *do* you need?"

"Who knows what I need."

"Does your wife know you're here?"

"She has an idea."

"What else does she have an idea of?" She narrowed her eyes. They looked black, but he knew they were blue.

"Are you trying to see into my soul?" he asked, edging towards her.

"Does it bother you?"

"I don't mind."

"Tell me more things like I'm a dark princess."

"I don't know what else you are."

"Make it up." The skin of her neck and chest shone with moisture. The dimple in her chin only showed when the light skimmed across her in the right way. He wondered if there was a little gap between her front teeth. He watched her lips, willing them to part for a second so he could see.

"Teach me how to do it," he said.

"What?"

"To see into people's souls."

"So you can see inside me?"

"Yea."

"It doesn't work on me."

"Just teach me."

"Or we could talk normally."

"I'm not good at normal."

She took a step back. He wondered if he should tell her the reason for his fascination, or would that break the spell? He reached out to take her hand; she gripped back for a few seconds and then let go.

"I'm not good at normal either," she said and slipped into the crowd. Even through the happy swirl he felt it – something tugging at him, a lonely message that made less sense with every step she took away.

9

Disability

RUTH WAS IVY'S SISTER. She had just turned eighteen and was engaged to be married that autumn. The excitement made her even louder than usual. She sat opposite Ivy, bobbing around as she spoke.

"I don't want one of those dresses that take up the whole aisle, that's stupid. I see these women – their groom can't even reach them. Do you think I should get a fitted dress? But should it be white? It has to be white! A fitted dress that's not white wouldn't even be a wedding dress. But maybe that would be better. But what if a bird shits on me on the way in? It would be better white if that happened. If that happened though, oh my God!"

The train had stopped and people around them were eavesdropping, some more subtly than others.

"That's not going to happen." Ivy replied vacantly.

"How do you know?"

"Get one of those parasols to carry, just in case."

"Yea. But they're stupid."

"A bird won't do that to you."

"Do what to me?"

"Shit on you."

"Haha sorry, I just wanted to hear you swear, it sounds so funny."

"Why?"

"Cos you never swear!"

"Don't I?"

"You never swear. When Milo fucks you you're probably like, *Oh my! Goodness! Oh that's splendid.*"

"I do my share, don't worry."

Ruth smirked. "Well, glad he's giving you *something*."

"… Dresses."

"I wasn't going to talk about him. But yea, dresses …" When she spoke again the whole carriage heard. "I hate trains!" The man next to her gave a little smile of agreement without looking up from his book. "They're always full of people and their BO." She shuffled impatiently. "Look at these grease patches on the windows. They're so nasty. Someone should clean them." Ivy noticed a round smear on the glass next to her where someone had leant their head. "It's always there. Always! People need to have a shower! How's the class doing? How's that crawling one, what's his name?"

"Carne."

"Carne. You're bound to be strange with a name like Carne."

"I quite like it."

"You like everything. What is going on with this train!?"

They had been sitting still for a long time with no announcement. People rustled their newspapers and glanced accusingly at the speakers above them.

"Yea, anyway," Ruth continued, "if you're called Jack or something, I think you'll probably grow into a Jack. Jack the Lad or whatever. Or if you're called something weird like Carne or … I dunno, something weird. I can't think of anything…"

"I know what you mean."

The train was busy, a few people stood over them. A man let go of the pole he had been gripping and stood with his hands in his pockets. He was handsome and smug. Ivy watched him discretely, hoping the train would jerk back into motion and topple him over.

"How's the rest of the class?"

"Ok. Some are sweethearts, some need a slap."

"I bet."

"I feel clueless every day, one way or another."

"You'll be amazing. You were made to be a teacher."

"If you say so."

"You taught me loads of stuff." She poked Ivy's knee. "Like how to piss off Mum." Their mother had been almost as horrified with Ruth's fiancé as she had been with Milo. He was a thirty nine year old surgeon who rented a different car every month and talked about appendectomies at the dinner table. "You're patient. All good teachers are patient."

"People keep telling me I'm patient."

"Cos you are! You don't even seem to mind that this FUCKING TRAIN isn't moving!"

"Why do you think we're not moving?"

"Nearly ten minutes you know," an elderly woman put in, tutting and pointing to the watch she wasn't wearing.

"Typical! Isn't it? Typical!" grumbled a man in paint-stained dungarees.

Ivy examined the people around her and their growing impatience. A few had struck up conversations, complaining and chuckling in a rare moment of mutual acknowledgement. They were underground and the windows showed nothing but the darkness of the tunnel and their faint reflections. Three men entered from the next car and ploughed their way through the commuters. There was an expectant hush in case they brought an explanation. The lights flickered above. The men said nothing and passed into the next carriage, slamming the door behind them. Ruth was sitting in a fidgety silence. The light flickered again and then went out, one carriage at a time. With the darkness came an eruption of whispers. After a few seconds the light returned. No one was reading anymore, no one was talking.

When they creaked back into motion those with newspapers went back to reading them and everyone else glazed over. The man standing with his hands in his pockets was jolted but caught himself easily. Ivy looked at herself in the glass. Her eyes were black against the background of the tunnel, her dark red hair messed up from her own meddling. A few stops later they got off and walked to the restaurant.

The two of them had monthly lunches together, a tradition they had kept up in recent years. Husbands and boyfriends were forbidden. This month it was more essential than ever. Ivy had been lacking in adult company, but for staff room chat and the odd appearance from Milo. Ruth wittered away, projecting above the clang and bustle of the open kitchen. She wore a thin braided headband and a sleeveless top to show off the tattoo she regretted. She was shorter than her sister and darker from a sunbed habit.

"Ivy ... Why are you staring at me like a perv?"

Ivy had been watching her placidly, saying nothing.

"I was just thinking it's a shame we only get together once a month."

"Do you need to be rescued? Sorry. You're right. We could do something, once everything's settled." The wine waiter came over to fill their glasses.

"Once you're a married woman and need rescuing too," Ruth was about to retort, but instead just zipped two fingers across her lips. "How is Greg, anyway?"

"The same oaf he always is. How's your one?" The waiter returned and Ruth sang a "thank you", taking the plates before he could put them down. Ivy took a bite and began again.

"When we ruin our lives and scare all the men away we should live together. And be spinsters."

"We can't be spinsters cos we're both married, dumbo. But we could be divorcees."

"Or widows."

"Err ok ... I wouldn't blame you."

"I don't know where that came from."

"If you want to murder Milo, you have my full support."

"Thanks."

Ruth twizzled her spaghetti, then asked more quietly.

"Why *did* you get married so young?"

"Because I thought I knew better than everyone."

"You never seemed like a diehard romantic."

"Didn't I?"

"Maybe you were, but you kept it from me because you're a big sister and everything."

"You don't seem like one either."

"Romance makes me cringe."

The restaurant was bright and busy. Their table sat next to a set of French windows opening onto a small square of green. They often came here so they could people-watch and Ruth could speak loudly without irritating anyone.

"We're very different people, Ruth. You don't need to be afraid of anything."

"What's that supposed to mean?"

"If you mess it up you'll do it in your own way."

Ruth swallowed her mouthful. "What I mean is … Why did we both decide to get married young?"

"I've told you my reason."

"That's not a real reason though. You knew *what* better than everyone?"

"I really don't know. I just wanted to surprise myself."

"And did it work?" A table at the far end of the restaurant began singing a raucous happy birthday.

"Yes … You know when people say they feel brand new. It was that."

"Can I tell you a secret."

"What?"

"I have no idea why I'm doing this." Ivy straightened her fork and posture, ready to be sensible. "Don't get me wrong. I'm loving it … Do you remember when we were kids and Mum made us do those tennis classes?"

"Sure."

"Remember when we were practising our footwork or whatever and I turned on the ball-shooting machine at the instructor?"

"Ha! Yea."

"And that fat little girl told on me. I was near the socket where it was plugged in and I just pressed it before I could think."

"Naughty child."

"This is going to sound a bit far out." She put her cutlery down. "When I asked Greg to marry me, it was the same."

"You did it without thinking?"

"It sounds messed up. But I just let the words slip out. What's wrong with me?"

"Are you happy?"

"Sooo happy."

"Sooo … there you go."

Ruth peered around the room from table to table. "I'm so happy I can't do anything. It's like a disability. I can't concentrate."

"Lucky you don't have a job then."

Ruth giggled inanely then suddenly stopped. "Am I sane?"

"Everyone's a bit mad, Ruth."

"I suppose."

"I wouldn't worry. If you want actual mad, go and talk to that metal man back there." She gestured to the street they'd come from.

"I've heard about him … Tell me honestly though. How long does it last for?" Ivy swirled her glass. "I mean … It can't last for more than a few months. It's not normal. The other day I cried watching some gardening programme. When the old woman came home and she was so happy because her garden was nice. I was crying and thinking *Wow, I'm a loser.*"

Ivy laughed. "I don't think I've ever had that. For me it was just simple and special, like I was walking around with a secret."

"I know that bit. The secret bit. It doesn't stay secret for long though, I blurt it out all over the place."

"I've noticed."

On their way back to the train station they saw him again. Ruth was darting ahead through the crowd with Ivy pacing to keep up. He was stood still amid all the movement in his usual pose. *There's a man in there*, Ivy reminded herself as the sun flashed off his armour and their heels clipped on past.

10

Our missing man

THE CLASSROOM WAS EMPTY. Ivy sat with a pair of scissors held next to her cheek, looking at the display boards. They were bare but for old staples and shreds of paper. She had still not filled them despite their ugly presence reminding her every day. The evening outside was growing dismal; rain buffeted on the windows, obscuring the view. Someone's jumper lay squashed under the leg of a chair, caked in dust. Thirty unmarked spelling tests were piled in front of her, on top of them a scrap of paper she'd been writing on. The emptiness of the room and the clownish yellow of the walls kept her rigid, like an unforgiving audience. She rolled a strand of her hair between two fingers, snipping at the tips.

There was a brief knock and the door opened. It was the school secretary. Ivy had never remembered her name and now it was too late to ask. She was a flustered woman who wore floral dresses and drank obscene amounts of coffee.

"Need some help Ivy, my love. I was after Ms Haddow, but she's gone home."

"What's up?"

"I've got a kid of yours whose folks haven't showed up to take him home."

"Who?"

"Carne. I'll bring him over here if that's ok. I need to make some phone calls to track someone down. Can't get through to his father."

"What are you going to do?"

"Well we've got the address; we can try that if worst comes to worst. It's barely an hour since home time though, so not yet. I'll do some detective work."

"Ok. Bring him here, that's fine."

Carne made his way to the far corner and climbed up into a chair.

"Do you want something to eat?" He ignored her and squeaked the soles of his shoes on the floor. She searched for more to say, grateful for an excuse to procrastinate. "You'll ruin your shoes doing that, you know." He didn't answer; boys don't care about their shoes. She turned back to her paper just as he squeaked again. What did boys like? "There was a massive frog in my house the other day."

From across the room he glanced up then replied scathingly, "No there wasn't."

"There was. It was asleep on the sofa, but I opened the curtains and gave it a fright."

"No there wasn't. Frogs need water. They wouldn't be on your sofa. They'd dry out." Another squeak.

"Really it was my husband. He reminds me of a frog. He's lazy."

"Frogs aren't lazy." His responses were swift and irritable.

"Do you like frogs then?" He didn't answer. Ivy put the scissors down and returned to her paper, (*chain-smoking tramp* or just *chain smoker?*) She ignored the squeaks in the hope that he would get bored.

He didn't. "Don't do that please, Carne."

"What?"

"Squeak your shoes against the floor."

"I can't help it."

"Don't be a twit. I've got work to do and it's bad for your shoes."

"They're itchy." He crouched forward, wiping both feet against the floor one after the other.

"Then take your shoes off and scratch them."

"My shoe's itchy, not my foot." He squeaked again, chuffed with his own humour.

She tried a different tack. "Carne. Have you heard the story about the boy who squeaked his shoes?"

"No."

"One day there was a boy …"

"I bet it's rubbish."

"… who rubbed his shoes against the floor so much that he wore through the soles of his shoes until he had no shoes. Then he rubbed his feet on the floor till he wore through those too. Finally when he had no feet left …"

"That would take ages."

"Yes. He didn't stop, he kept doing it forever."

"What an idiot."

"He wasn't an idiot. He was a very clever boy. People just thought he was stupid because he squeaked his shoes."

"You don't think I'm stupid though. You told me I'm a clever one."

"I'm not talking about you."

"Why did you tell me the story then?"

"Sometimes, when I talk to you Carne … I don't feel like I'm talking to a little boy." His restless form slowed and he shot her a look of cautious gratitude, then squeaked again.

"His shoes wouldn't wear through anyway. Just the bottom bit. How can you wear through the top bit with the laces?"

"I suppose … he just rubbed them too much." She tried to make her answer light-hearted, as though she were bantering with a friend. This annoyed him more.

"That's not true either. Nothing you say is real." He rubbed his shoe harder but it made no sound. Frustrated, he repeated until it came.

"Carne, don't be so rude."

"Don't tell me stupid lies then."

What time was it? Various scenarios occurred to her: Carne's father snoozing on the pavement outside a pub or trapped under the wreckage in a road accident, twisted metal spearing his body, whispering his son's name on the threshold of death.

"I know you're worried about your Dad." He sniggered and tipped onto the back legs of his chair. From here on he ignored everything she said. After a few more attempts she returned to her paper, defeated. Another twenty minutes passed. Carne got bored of squeaking his shoe and started blowing long wet raspberries. Another half hour later, when he had fallen asleep on his folded arms, the door opened.

"We found our missing man." It was the triumphant secretary, followed by a wiry man in a dark suit. Carne's head raised and lowered into his arms again.

"Wonderful of you all. Saints, you're saints, and I'm a scoundrel. Aha."

"It's not us you need to apologise to. It's lucky he didn't leave on his own."

"Ah, there's more where he came from. You must be Miss Blakely?" He extended his hand. She shook it only after a deliberate pause.

"Mrs."

"Mrs Blakely. Peter Hansel. Or Pepper, as in a peck of pickled. Carne loves you, he's told me about you. He loves you."

"He loves me, does he?" she replied with amusement.

"Loves you and now I love you."

The secretary knocked and said goodbye. Ivy thanked her, emphasising the difficulty of it all.

"You ok there, boyo?" The boy nodded and descended from the chair. "Suppose I owe you a cake or something," Pepper reached down to him. "Mrs Blakely once again, thank you. Now I have my son, my son has a cake, and you have your peace and quiet. Everybody is happy." He did a little bow to her and turned to leave.

"Where were you?" she called out as he passed through the doorway.

He turned back around. "You would never believe me if I told you. Aha."

11

Poor Milo

THERE WERE PENNIES STUCK to the ceiling. A prior generation of pennies, now obsolete. Milo inspected them with his head back and a hissing in his ears. A fork hung loosely in his hand with a mouthful of steak – long ago gone cold – stuck in the prongs. He was zipped up in his jacket despite the mild weather. He hadn't eaten for days, spurred on only by tiptoe and grim determination. The hissing was temporary; his eardrums would spasm in relief for a few hours and then go back to normal. It was like a thin wall of sound insulating him from the humdrum of reality, just when he needed it most. A large mirror hung on the wall ahead of him. The top half of his head showed in the glass, just above the frame. He needed a haircut. In three minutes his shift would start and he would not be there. His disappearance would begin. A few tables along, a family sat with straight backs and paper napkins tucked into their collars. By their feet a brown Labrador begged and sulked with every bite they took.

Why had he ordered a steak of all things? It was tough and called for energy his jaw didn't have. The mushrooms were easier; he worked on those. After getting lost in the crowd the only sign of Aaron was a goodbye text in the morning. Milo danced on for another day and night and made his own way back.

Out the window the traffic had come to a stop. Someone blasted repetitive music from their car as though personally for Milo, to remind him where he had been. On the far side of the road by the train station a fruit seller was yelling out his bargains. Every so often a clatter of glasses at the bar left Milo shuddering internally. He needed a thicker insulation: a duvet, forgetfulness – soon enough. Maybe the pub would have rooms upstairs. If he lived through the steak he would find out. He took another bite.

The three minutes were gone, he was officially skipping work. Until now no-one would have missed him. Almost no-one. The way Ivy missed him had changed. She used to be indignant about it. Now she missed him idly, like good weather. In the course of their marriage he had disappeared three times. He cut a corner of the steak and picked it up in his fingers. The dog's ears twitched. Milo looked in its soppy eyes, encouraging. It plodded over and chomped.

A few years ago a stray dog had followed him around for a whole day. He was on holiday, sitting on a bench by the sea, when it approached him. From there to the supermarket and a restaurant and then in the evening to the hotel, it trod along behind him, waiting outside for him to finish at every stop. When he emerged from the hotel the next day, Milo half-expected to see it still there, but it was gone. He hadn't fed it a morsel. There was nothing in his life he regretted more. The family looked in his direction; he ignored them and cut another chunk for his new friend.

"I'm going to make you into a big bad wolf," he said to it. "The vegetables are for me through."

His phone buzzed with a message from Aaron: *Disappearing again??*

He tore the remainder of the steak in two halves, throwing one to the dog and keeping the rest for himself. "That's all you're getting." It scoffed happily.

Disappearance number four. Fourth time lucky? If he could finish this meal without vomiting that would be lucky enough for now.

"Single or double room?"

"Single."

"Just as well, I'm not sure if there's a double for you."

"Ok."

"This is a family establishment, you see." The landlord spoke without looking up from the pint he was pulling. His short hairy forearms poked out from the bottom of a gaudy checkered shirt. A large brown blotch covered three quarters of his head, poorly hidden by wisps of feathery white hair. "You didn't like the steak?"

"It was tough, but ok."

He passed the pint to a customer and turned to open the till. "So you want to stay with us do you?"

"Us? Can I have a whisky before I go up?"

"You seem a bit out of the ordinary. If you don't mind me saying so." Milo laughed, despite his feeble state. The landlord shared a smile. "What brand?"

"Anything."

He took a glass and poured a generous measure straight from the bottle. "You're not supposed to do that anymore. Supposed to use the measures. I think it takes the soul out."

"I can keep a secret."

The man's face was puffy and his nose red with burst capillaries. As he handed over the whisky he inspected Milo, from his missing shirt buttons to his wired pupils. "I can too. But don't give me any, if you don't mind… How long do you want to stay?"

"I don't know yet."

"We ask people to pay in advance, you see."

"Ok, five nights."

"Shall I show you the room first?"

"As long as it's got a bed I don't care."

"No bags?"

"Nope."

Upstairs, a single light bulb led their way along the corridor. Rows of still-life pictures hung along the faded pink wallpaper.

"You met the Waivers – the pup at least." He pointed to the first door as he said this. Milo's mouth was dry and sour with whisky aftertaste. The landlord placed one foot in front of the other with a leisurely precision, introducing each door as they went. "In there lives a man and his wife by the name of Sanderson. Don't leave the room much. Mr Jacob is in there, he's barely ever here. Workman, doesn't need sleep." They turned the corner to see the hallway extending twice as far again. Milo dragged his heel and stumbled. "Don't lie down yet. Nearly there. That room's full of junk, don't worry about that one."

"I'm not worrying," Milo replied dryly.

"In there is Baby and Isa. Woman called Baby, there's a first time for everything. Young couple. Strange ones, you might like them."

"I might know them."

"You know them? We'll knock …" He sidestepped and raised a fist.

"Not now. Not now. I have to sleep. Come on."

"Suit yourself. Don't be a stranger though. We're not fond of strangers."

This part of the corridor was even dimmer; the walls seemed to close in on them as they walked.

"Mrs McDuff lives in there. And our last stop …" He turned the key and sunlight beamed across the floorboards. Milo had half-forgotten it was daytime. "Happy recovery."

Where do you go when you disappear? He sank through the thin pillow to the springs of the mattress beneath, bidding one goodnight to everything. The swivelling office chair, the beeping calls, the concerned faces searching him for clues, what was really wrong with him, that he needed to do what he did? Goodnight to the unconcerned faces, gurning away on the dance floor. Goodnight *Poor Milo. Poor Milo?* Is that what she said? He jolted and the sun was gone. But it wasn't all a dream. Poor Milo, with a wife who loves him. He was sweating. He'd fallen asleep with all his clothes on, even his shoes. The bed squeaked as he undressed. Two identical women, one in love with him and one a stranger – he'd never been good at riddles.

The next time he woke it wasn't as abrupt. The darkness and quiet were deeper and all that remained of the riddle was her shimmering hot skin, her jumbled red hair, and someone new to fall in love with him all over again. Sylvie. Second Chance Sylvie. It sounded like an antidote.

Nothing relieved the tiredness. His heartbeat still thumped incessantly, like the bass lines he had come here to escape. His phone was buried in clothes. Without it the time was only night. But which night? *He's gone again,* she'd be thinking. Growing cynical, but too stubborn to fall out of love. Second chance Sylvie. Third chance who? Fifth chance, last chance who? They'd never run out or else life would run out first. It sounded melancholy – was that the drugs?

12

You and me

AARON'S UN-GELLED HAIR hung low over his forehead. He was slouched in the middle of the sofa, shoes off, socked foot pawing at Ivy's coffee table.

"I want us to share what we know. Not that I know very much." He was struggling.

"What have you got to tell me?"

"Whenever Milo does one of his runners I always know. He tells me. And he'll act restless and moan more than usual. I don't know where, but I always know he's going. This time he just seemed normal. He mentioned nothing and now he's gone."

"We should keep a leash on him."

"I'm not saying we should go to the police."

"One of those black collars with the spikes."

"…Just that we should be thinking where he might be."

"I have been thinking."

"Yes?"

"Yea. I think a lot. It doesn't get me anywhere. I think I should get dumber, dumb people are happier right?"

"I wouldn't know about that," he replied with a goofy smile that vanished quickly.

"I don't care if he comes back, Aaron. It's his choice."

"That's what I'm saying! If it was his choice he would have told me."

"How do you know?"

"I know."

"He's secretive. More than you know. More than I do probably."

"Ok. How about this … And don't take this the wrong way." Ivy stiffened up for an insult. "He did some really … unfair things to you."

"You think?" She couldn't quite keep the kink out of her voice.

"… But, did he ever try that hard to keep it from you? I mean, he didn't tell you to your face obviously."

"He did actually."

"Ok he did … sometimes. And other times he just made it so you knew without saying it …"

"Me on the other hand …"

"The point isn't you. The point is he's too much of a blockhead to keep secrets properly. We would have known if something was wrong. He's not the type to just …"

"What type is he, Aaron?"

"I'm not trying to fight you, I'm just worried."

"Me too."

"Yea?"

"I'm worried that he'll come back. I'm worried he'll be stuck to me forever."

"Well … maybe. But it would be good to know he's safe."

Ivy laughed. "When did you become such a saint? I know you remember."

"This isn't about me … Or you and me." On opposite sofas they regarded each other, a moment's recognition cutting through. A square of sun lit up the carpet and the crisps of leaf walked in from the street.

13

Leaves

"MISS, YOU LOOK FUNNY TODAY." The children filed into the classroom. All but one girl, who squinted up at her waiting for an answer.

"Thank you. That's the look I was going for … Sit down will you." The girl complied only after examining her a bit longer. Ivy was faint with tiredness.

As the morning progressed the class became abnormally quiet, their muttering no louder than their scribbling. This was a delicate peace that could be broken at any moment; even a cough could upset the balance. She walked between the desks, treading carefully. Their task was to complete an unfinished story. It was about a girl called Sonia who kept finding leaves in suspicious places around her house. She peered over the first shoulder:

Sonia went to the shed and the shed was dark and she was scard and the rake was scard too cos he was cort with the leafs. What are you doing putting leafs in the house sed sonia. It wasnt me said the rake. why do you have leafs then said sonia. I was pratsing for when i get to rake sed the rake and Soni was angry and she punch the rake in the face and the rake starts crying and sed it was the brush did it and the brush said it was the rake and only blaming him becos he knows he done it cos he was a rake anyway. so the rake punch the brush in face and the bristols fell out and then the lonmower got angry becos he was sleeping and everyone shouting and then they all got frends agen. The end.

"So who did it, Charlie?"

Charlie was stretching proudly to show he had finished.

"It was the brush but he blamed the rake."

"You don't say that though, do you?"

"But they're all friends, so it doesn't matter."

"I suppose not. Do you know where Hector is today?"

"No ... Miss."

She continued, searching for someone whose handwriting she could read. Bunmi had written nearly a page in large loopy font.

Sonia went to the forest sometimes and one time she met a man and fell in ...

There was a gasp as chairs clattered into each other. Two boys rolled onto the floor, swinging their arms wildly. She heard a thump and a cry. Children clambered over desks to see what was going on. Ivy darted through. Just before she pulled them apart, she saw Carne baring his teeth as his fist clunked into the boy's cheek.

"Get off him! Get ..." Carne's arms relaxed and he let himself be dragged away. The other boy looked around in shock, his cheek beginning to swell and his lips blubbering. "You've done it this time Carne! Stay there!" She yanked him into the corner of the room, scraping his knees across the carpet. Carne sat back against the wall, studying her with a scrunched brow. "Face the wall!" He stayed where he was, his cheeks stiff with resentment. "Face the wall!" Behind her the class were howling like animals. Carne refused to move. "Ok fine. Don't face the wall. I'll tell Ms Lobo you were fighting in my class and then you disobeyed me. You're in big trouble Carne. Now face the wall!" He glared at her and held his position. Ivy swivelled around to see thirty children screaming and stumbling around in excitement. Carne's adversary was on the floor, stunned and bleeding. For a second she hesitated, unsure whether to help him first or control the class. "EVERYBODY SIT DOWN! I'M GOING TO COUNT TO THREE! ONE ..." The boy was prodding at his injury. "TWO ..." She realized this was the one boy whose name she had not yet remembered. "THREE ..." The noise mostly died down, but for a low chattering and scraping of chairs. As she approached the boy, she was shaking visibly. "Let me see." The skin was pink and puffed up. "Charlie, go and get Ms Hadow!" Charlie trotted to the door followed by two friends. "Only Charlie! Someone get me a chair!" She regretted saying this as the class erupted again competing to get a chair. "You'll be fine honey. It's just a bruise." She sat him down.

"What have we here? Someone got themselves in a squabble?" Ms Haddow tilted the boy's head from side to side, inspecting the damage. "What was all that about Aiden? Eh?"

Aiden – that was his name. Ivy stood to one side allowing Ms Hadow to scoop the boy up and lead him out of the room.

"Sit down Charlie." Charlie had been hovering next to her. "And everyone else, sit down! And calm down."

Before returning to his table, Charlie cast a cautious glance past her to the far wall, then back to her. In an effort to restore peace Ivy stood still, glaring from one child to another. A hush returned. Bunmi was looking past her at the far wall just as Charlie had done. Others were doing the same. How long had they known, she wondered as she turned and saw that Carne was gone.

"He wouldn't have just hit you for no reason." Aiden shrugged and wriggled in his seat. It was lunchtime, he sat in front of Ivy holding an ice pack to his face. "So? What did you say?"

"Nothing."

"So you were sitting there doing your work and Carne hit you?"

"We were talking, but normally. Then he got angry."

"What were you talking about?"

"Just normal things, I wasn't cussing him."

"What were you talking about?"

"I was just joking." He wouldn't look at her. "He hit me first. I just pushed him back when he pushed me. He should be in trouble not me."

"Carne is in trouble, believe me."

"He's the one you should be telling off."

"Aiden … just be honest with me. Do you know what honest means?"

"Yes."

"What does it mean?"

"Telling the truth."

"Do you think we can be honest with each other? The sooner I know what happened the sooner you can have your lunch."

"I'm not hungry."

Ivy sat back and sighed. She was hungry. The nerves had settled, leaving her weak and unfocused. The school secretary had phoned Mr Hansel. Teachers were searching the school grounds for the missing boy. All Ivy wanted was to be left alone.

"Aiden, just tell me what happened. You're not going anywhere till you do." Aiden sniffed and shook his head. "Fine. Wait here." She got up and left the classroom.

Outside Charlie was chewing on a sandwich with his mouth open. "Charlie, thanks for waiting. I…"

"It's ok."

"Thanks. I want you to tell me what happened between Carne and Aiden."

"They had a fight."

"How did it start?"

"They got angry and started fighting. And Aiden's face broke."

"Who started it?"

"I don't know, I think they both started it."

"Charlie, it's important you tell me the truth. This is serious."

"I don't know; they were sitting, then they were on the floor like brrbbbrrrbbrrbrbbpubbup-pap-pap-pap!" Charlie mimed the punches.

"What were they talking about?"

"About you."

"Me?" Charlie nodded. "What about me?"

"Aiden said you looked like a witch and Carne said that's not what witches look like and Aiden said how would you know and Carne said I just know and Aiden said it's just cos you love Miss Blakely and Carne said shut up I don't love her and Aiden said you love her and then they were fighting."

"Who touched who first?" Ivy sorely wished the headmistress were here to help, this was headmistress territory.

"I don't know. They both went mad."

"Charlie, Ms Lobo is going to be back in tomorrow and Ms Lobo can tell if you're lying."

"I'm not lying. It might have been Carne. I think it might have been but I don't know. It might have been Aiden as well though. I don't know."

"Do you promise you're telling the truth?" He did an exaggerated nod. "Is Carne your friend?"

"No."

"Why not?" He shrugged and bit into his sandwich. "We need to find out where Carne's gone, Charlie. Or we're all in trouble. Is there a hiding place you know he might be in?"

"I don't know."

"Who is Carne's friend?"

"Carne doesn't have friends. He's angry cos he has to crawl like a bug."

"That's enough. Who does he talk to the most?"

"Hector."

"Who else?" He shrugged again. Ivy looked up and down the corridor, at the display boards and the floor smeared with lines from rubber shoes. No-one was here to help. Everyone who was free was out searching for Carne. "Ok, off you go." Charlie scampered towards the playground.

Back in the classroom Ivy collapsed into her chair. She was so drained she probably did look like a witch.

"Do you want some more ice?"

"No."

"So, I'm a witch am I?"

Aiden blinked irritably. "What do you mean?"

"Aiden, I don't mind. I can take it. I just want to know what happened. I'm bored of all this."

"He hit me. That's what happened. Tell him off."

"Why did you tell Carne he loved me? Were you trying to make him look silly?"

"No."

"No, what?"

"I said it cos it's true. Everyone knows he loves you. He gets angry when people say it."

"Well ... so you said it to make him angry?"

"He hit me! Tell him off!" His chin quivered.

"When we find Carne, he'll be in a lot of trouble."

"Find him then!"

"Don't raise your voice Aiden. We're doing our best. Now tell me, is there anywhere in this school where children hide?"

"Dunno."

"Aiden?"

"I promise I don't know. Can I go to lunch now?"

"I thought you weren't hungry." She slumped back and looked at the high beams of the ceiling. The room had once been a chapel, long ago. She cleared her throat. "Go."

14

The Beetle

SHE HAD LEFT QUIETLY. The panic and tears lasted only a few days and were followed by an all-encompassing resignation. Roan had immersed himself in television, half asleep all the time but aiming for an hour of daylight every day at least through the window. He was not in tune with himself and this awareness haunted him. One night he woke up twitching and shivering. Another night he wept until he could barely breathe. But most nights passed uneventfully and he grew to love the walls of his flat. Months passed and he began to wonder what would be the most appropriate way, if he were to go mad. How did people usually go mad?

For a while he examined his hairline compulsively; it seemed to recede further as evening approached. Music annoyed him. It seemed to be mocking him. Every note took a sarcastic twist. Animal documentaries fascinated him, although this was nothing new. He would watch whole box sets at once, thinking about the life he might see out of each pair of eyes. For a long time he had no sex drive at all. Gradually it came back, but he was left feeling like an old man and pursuing new women seemed ridiculous. He spent his fortieth birthday in bed, forcing himself back to sleep again and again.

In a way it had been comforting to believe that a devil had possessed him; it seemed romantic. A deep shame filled him when the phone rang unanswered. One night he picked up the receiver and heard his mother on the other end. Why had he ignored so many calls? They spoke for nearly an hour and scheduled to meet up the following day. Roan didn't make the appointment, intending to call back when the chirp had returned to his voice. From then on he was left alone by everyone but Pepper, who berated him with advice and stories and occasionally money for his projects. Since they first met Pepper had seen him go from an actor to a street mime to a professional statue, commending every transformation.

Gradually Roan brought himself back. The sleeping pattern he lived by became more regular. Before long only the boredom remained and even this went away at last. Dreams had always been an interest of his and now they became a lifeline: a language to practise on his own, to keep from going mute. When he looked in the mirror these days he made an effort to leave his hair line alone. If he sensed a wave of negativity he would swallow it up, accepting it with a feigned philosophical air. Occasionally he would slip into a quiet despair but this rarely lasted more than a few hours. Most of the time this happened on his days off, when he would wake up as late as he could and then slowly paw over his breakfast trying to decide how to spend the day.

Something very sour had pervaded his dream. Just a few moments ago he had wakened and reached for the notebook in an effort to snatch it before it was gone. Some creature he had chased with an upside-down glass too small to cover it and his own legs too slow to catch it. Now it was under the bed or behind the wardrobe, somewhere, lurking to scurry out once he was asleep again. Writing them down often prevented dreams from coming back; he was not sure why this was. Examination seemed to dissolve them. This was sad sometimes, to write words describing what could never exist again. He had got used to writing in the dark. Turning on the light distracted him and dragged his mind into daytime mode. Writing in the dark was good for dream memory and by now he could always keep it legible and often within the lines.

As a child, when he woke up with nightmares his mother used to take him to the bathroom and tell him to throw the bad dream down the toilet. He made scooping motions with his hand and threw a ball of air into the toilet bowl and flushed. As he fell back asleep, his mother would tell him a story just to keep the fear at bay.

Roan levered himself to the side of the bed and switched on the light. When the dazzle had passed he stood up and tiptoed through the paper city. He opened the curtains, searching for signs of the dawn and just about saw it, a glow at the base of the sky, mostly blocked by the houses. He turned his attention to a pair of beetles on the windowsill outside, trundling slowly over the cracked paint. He angled his nails against the glass and scratched. These little balls of black with scurrying legs, they were filling him. Dreams are beetles, his dreams at least. An irritation followed, itching in his rib cage. He pursed his lips to the where the small creatures were walking and spat. His saliva dripped down the glass and pooled at the bottom. Outside they plodded on regardless. As quickly as it had arisen, the irritation was gone and he reached for a tissue to clean up. He opened the window and put his arm on the far side, keeping it there until the first of the beetles clambered onto his finger. It was so alien. How could this thing belong in the same patch of space and time as he did? Outside there was no wind. The temperature was so neutral he could barely feel his own skin. The beetle sat motionless, coiled into itself like a child hiding behind his own hands in a game of hide and seek. How would it be to have the ground beneath your feet lift you up and examine you? Every wall, pavement or building might be poised to squash you. He hated the weakness of this creature, this helpless thing frozen between fight and flight. With another finger he pressed lightly on its arched back. It scrabbled to escape, but he had it trapped.

For a few more moments he savoured the possibility of the imminent death he could inflict. A whole existence, a small ignorant life here or nowhere, it was up to him. If dreams were beetles then what was this one about? It was too powerless to be a nightmare. He loosened his grip around the creature, just enough to feel its legs wiggling. This was an urgent dream; something small needed so badly. The notebook was still by his bed; he fetched it, taking care to keep a gentle grip on his captive. With his left hand he wrote:

- *Urgency*
- *Powerlessness*
- *Lifted up by a big hand*

This was enough for now. The rest was too unformed to write. As he released his beetle dream a thought struck him. This little thing would remain in his memory, while he, a giant made of the ground on which the beetle walked, who had held its life in the balance for a few moments, he would be forgotten. Beetles have no memory, he presumed, although he didn't know for certain. Surely they had none.

How could a huge man like him fit in such a tiny brain?

As morning came he still sat in his chair picking his teeth, feeling the dips at the root where his gums had receded. When he was bored with this he put each finger between his teeth one by one, biting down slowly, increasing the pressure until it started to hurt then moving to the next. He cracked his knuckles and dug his toes into the carpet wishing she would come and rescue him; wishing for anyone's company, even Pepper would do. What a common wish and how strange that he wished it so rarely. As he sat and stared she came to him, at the edge of his vision, patient and beautiful. Of course she was not really there. He was not so mad that every thought became a reality. Still, his thoughts were more solid than they used to be. The feel of her skin was not quite real, but it was enough. This was pleasantly warming and no more. He could not make her say anything, not without repeating memories, or putting words in her mouth. She stood there quietly, his own soft warm mannequin.

It was hunger that brought him back. He had finally transferred the groceries from the sofa to the fridge. The shelves were stuffed. Seeing this made the memories of the night fade. He took out half a jar of pasta sauce and a packet of ham, then microwaved and devoured them together. No longer hungry he returned to his chair.

"Did you … What shall I do for my next act? Standing around is getting boring." It took him a few words to work through the gravely texture of his voice. He did not talk enough and his vocal chords were getting weak. "I'm thinking some sort of … animal, alien but a bit more … You don't have to listen to me babble on." She had been by him while he ate, aglow with attentiveness but without intruding. Where had this new-found interest and patience come from? She had never been so happy to stand and listen when she was alive. "Why are you just standing there? Sit down." She sat down, stretching out her legs with a careless elegance. As he lay back next to her on the bed she snuggled into him, her curly blonde hair ruffling against his chest. It was so homely. With just the ease of a thought, he could move her body, bend her around and on top of him; he could touch her and spread her, make her quiver and moan. Soon enough. For now they just lay together. There was no hurry in this dimension.

At once he was restless. The tension jolted through her body from his. He comforted her and the peace returned. She was naked now. The warmth of her body seized him; a spurt of energy crossed through his stomach tasting of something delicious. With her feeble hands she pawed at the buttons of his shirt, unable to undo them.

Sprawled out naked on the bed he was alone again. She had gone, leaving him with teeth clenched and arms resting limply on his inner thighs. The bed was larger than usual; he had always suspected things were not as stable as they seemed. The bed had flourished and would soon shrink and this cycle of seasons would continue unnoticed by most. Right now the bed was at its largest, in its prime of summer, while he was at his weakest. Its fatherly grip held him above the floor, higher than usual. Slowly, by just a few inches, it was rising to fit into the enlarging room. The ceiling was so high it could have been the sky, were it not for the blotches of mould.

He knew what was happening and he didn't resist. The bed lifted him into the air, his acceptance speeding it up. Sheets crinkled around him as the mattress bent and he was enfolded. Peeping over the edge he saw how far he was from the ground. Above, a shiny scaled face examined him, craning down close. If Roan had stretched out his arm he could have stroked the pincers which jutted towards him curiously. The mattress squeezed around him tighter, pushing the wind out of his lungs. It didn't mean to hurt him, only to pin him in place.

There was a noise, shrill and unwelcome. Then a banging. Someone was at the door. The face was gone. The bell rang again. Then the knocking continued. He was about to run and open it when he realized he was still naked. For several moments he pussyfooted between the door and his pile of clothes, unsure of whether to ignore it. The knocking came again. He pulled on his jeans and undid the lock. A lopsided grin greeted him.

"Hello Mr Knight."

15

Magic tricks

"YOU CALLED FOR ME?" Pepper said, sidling past him into the flat.

"Called you how?"

"You wished I was here."

"How did you … ?"

"Aha! A trick. A trick. Don't rip your hair out. I'll tell you how it's done."

Roan closed the front door and guided his guest through the folded paper on the floor. "Can you see into my mind?" They sat down on opposite sides of the room.

"That heap of artistic bollocks? No thank you."

"How did you know that I …"

"Relax man! Listen to this. It's an old trick I used to do a while back. A party piece. You have to choose the right kind of person. I'd say *You there! I bet I can read your mind.* They'd say *Oh really, what am I thinking?* Most of them are shouting a big *Fuck you* in their heads." He bent forward towards the folded paper structures below him. "You're the same, Roan. I can guess at the kind of things you wish for. I hope I didn't freak you." Pepper was dressed in another dark, ill-fitting suit.

"No more than usual."

"Good man." He moved his hand, a bulging vein wriggled from side to side.

"So what now?" Roan ventured.

"What, what now?"

"What did you want to say now that you're here?"

"Aha! Roan, you don't have guests often do you?"

Roan rummaged through his pockets, without knowing why. "Are you working today?" he asked, finding them empty but for a few coppers.

"I work every day. New ideas, new tricks. There are no holidays for an active mind."

"I suppose not."

"So ... Do I get an explanation?" Pepper pointed to the folded papers by his feet.

"Just something to keep me busy."

"That all you're sharing?"

"It started as a paper house. I got a bit carried away."

"Building yourself a city, are you?"

"I can only keep going to the walls."

"It's quite an artwork."

"Thanks."

"You got any tenants?"

"I made people to go in them, you'll see if you look closely."

Pepper stooped further forward. "So you have."

Roan clambered noisily over the back of the sofa to the kitchen sink. "Tap water?"

"Why not? We only live once."

He filled two glasses and stretched over the papers to give one to Pepper.

"How's the dream journaling?"

Roan gulped down the whole glass and refilled it. "It's ok ... Listen, I've been meaning to say sorry for the other day."

"Which day was that?"

"When you took me to see the hospital. You were showing me somewhere important to you and all I could talk about was ..."

"Not to worry. Not to worry. I know you're lost in your dreams. I just speak and wait, knowing it will sink in later."

"Well it did sink in. And thank you for taking me there."

"Pleasure."

"What's in the bag?"

Pepper had a leather backpack propped against his shin. "Glad you asked. New tricks. Let me show you." He rummaged inside, retrieving a silver globe the size of his palm. "They work on a scale. Some people want to see tricks, some want to believe in magic – give 'em as much as they can stomach. This one is for the timid." He held the ball in one hand above another, as though he were about to drop and catch it. "You Roan, you want a bigger piece of the pie than most."

He opened his fingers, leaving the ball hanging suspended in the air between the two hands. "Not only that. I've noticed the more magic I learn, the less people trust me. Everyone but you. Why, I wonder?" Pepper put the upper hand behind his back. The ball spun slowly, inches above his open palm.

"Because I know they're all tricks."

Pepper replaced the ball in his backpack. "Magnets. If you ever don't know the answer, it's magnets. This one's slightly stranger." He picked up the bag, digging into the bottom of it. "I'm sparing you the showmanship, I hope you don't mind. This is a lazy rehearsal." He brought out a pair of navy blue cotton tubes, like cut-off sleeves. "You know they're all tricks. You know everything is a trick." He slid the sleeves over both his forearms. "So nothing shocks you. There are no clear edges in that world of yours, Roan. That's why I chose you." Pepper took a sip of his water, then crossed one of his forearms over the other. "What papers have you used to build these? I see writing on them."

"She used to write to me when I was on tour. I kept all her letters."

"A city built of love letters, Aha! I would expect no less." He lifted one forearm an inch up then dropped it down so it tapped against the other and slid through below it. "You're a walking fairy-tale, Roan."

"How did you do that?"

"Don't feign surprise. It doesn't suit you."

"What else do you have?"

"I have one that I made just for you."

"What's that?"

Pepper opened and closed his jaw, clicking his teeth together as if testing their firmness. "Where do you keep your dream journal?"

"By the bed over there."

"May I see it?" Roan tottered through the stepping stones of free carpet and returned with the notebook. "Why do you trust me, Roan?" he asked, making an expression Roan had never seen.

"Don't you expect me too?"

Pepper flicked through the pages backwards, the handwriting getting more dishevelled as he did. Finally he handed it back. "Write today's date and copy down the words I say." Pepper put his elbows on his knees and blew lightly, making the paper rustle. "First bullet point: Pepper takes out a small box and brings it to me. Second: Inside the box is a beetle. He places it on my arm." Roan scribbled to keep up. "Third…The beetle bites my arm and sucks my blood, growing bigger. Fourth: It grows until it's too big to fit on my arm, then falls to the floor and scurries out of sight. My arm is dripping. My blood is white. Fifth: Pepper is gone."

Roan stretched and replaced the book on the nightstand. This was strong – he had not written so much detail for weeks. He got out of bed and pulled the blind open; it took a few minutes for his eyes to open fully against the light.

16

Gin

IF IT'S RAINING I'LL BUY MORE TIPTOE … If it's clear I'll get drunk. Milo yanked the curtain to one side: stars – *Drink it is.* He bought a bottle of gin, a sandwich and a toothbrush and paste. On the walk back he hooped the plastic bag onto his wrist and ate breakfast. According to the date on his phone he had slept for three nights. This didn't surprise him. Just before he got back he stopped, his mouth full of half chewed food, gawping at the stars as if trying to provoke them. "Whatever I do tonight is your fault! Haha."

Straight gin is a better wake-up call than a cold shower, but he had both just to be sure. Under the water he sang laddishly, his glass within reach behind the shower curtain. Each sip shocked him out of tune so he had to re-remember what he was singing. As he hit a particularly high note someone banged through the wall.

"I'm sorrieeeeeeey," he sang to them, holding the note until it croaked away.

His underwear and socks smelled a bit too far-gone to wear, so he wore none. Wallet, phone, room key, a final swig and he left into the night. The pub was closing up as he passed the landlord, who greeted his arrival in mock amazement. His phone buzzed again. *If it's a call I'll answer … If it's a text I'll throw it in the river.* It was neither – his battery was going. A surprising number of people missed him. Even Nadine had resurfaced: *You've disappeared! U like doing that I hear … U no where I am, weirdo! X.* Others read similarly. A lot of friends and people from the call centre enquired after him. And Ivy of course.

He'd drunk enough to warm his limbs and clear the last of his hibernation, no more. As he crossed the bridge over the river he stopped in the middle, stretched his arms out and whooped into the open air and the two halves of the city. Just as he did a rowing boat, so small he could barely see it, emerged in the swell below.

"HELLO BOAT PEOPLE!" he roared at them. Something moved; it could have been a wave. When they were out of range he took out his mobile and balanced it on the railing. "I want you to fall," he said, "but I'm still nervous to see you at the edge." Just before he could seal its fate the screen flashed with a call and it vibrated itself over and shrank downwards like a firefly.

"Have you been drinking?"

"Nothing outrageous."

"ID? … Look at me. You've got friends inside?"

"Yep."

"Ok. Have a good night."

Milo tipped an invisible hat and strolled inside. Around the floor people swaggered to the cheesy pop music, in the later stages of drunkenness. Couples smooching sloppily, the shot glasses smacking down on the bar, the screeches and hoots – it all seemed vulgar compared to the Hospital. The energy made him feel sober and self-conscious for a moment. He ploughed through a group of men in matching shirts to the bar, catching the server's attention before anyone else.

"Err… I was first?" a woman next to him protested.

"I've been like, totally here the whole time," Milo yelled back, mimicking her accent.

"Dickhead!"

"Do you want to touch it?" He pointed to his head and spluttered at his own wit. She leant forward over the bar holding a banknote. Her dress hugged the tops of her thighs. He drank his shot of gin and chased it with a mouthful of gin and tonic. The comforting bubble of tipsiness returned and he edged back, belching to himself and grinning manically. The woman beside him rotated her body lazily to the music, still trying to catch the barman's attention.

"Oh, you were waiting?" he asked, as if everything suddenly made sense. She ignored him. "I thought you were just standing there enjoying yourself." She spared him a brief, confused glance and edged away by the few spare inches available. Knowing she was still aware of him, he put down his drink and lurched towards her with his fingers splayed on either side of his head. She jolted and lost her footing, stumbling against the people behind her. Milo howled with laughter, took another swig and made for the dance floor.

The crowds were thicker here. He used his weight to lever his way through. The gin-smile was uncontainable. He really ought to drink gin more often. A line of girls acted out some joint dance moves. Someone bumped into him, spitting an apology in his ear. By the wall was a row of tables with sofas and buckets for champagne. A man in a suit was asleep, squidging out his double chin. A couple sat next to him rubbing each other under the table. Milo tapped his foot, feeling small. A vista opened, revealing a woman. She was tanned and nonchalant, with a low-cut blue dress and wavy hair. He battled his way through and then noticed her hand in someone else's. Too late.

"Hi! I'm Milo."

The man next to her adjusted his footing, other people around seemed to notice as well. The girl glanced around her as though searching for guidance, then turned back to him. "Hi," she replied cagily but he saw what he was searching for – an involuntary widening of her eyes, a flash of curiosity. He edged closer and spoke into her ear. "Is it horrible that I want to steal you?" He interlocked his fingers with hers, close against her hip, hidden from the man at her other side. Again he felt small as her protector and his friends closed in around him, like a moving forest. He ignored everyone but her. She pulled her hand free but couldn't stop looking at him.

There was a thud and his vision flashed. His cheek was aching and he knew why. What a weak punch for such a tall man: he had barely moved from the impact. The crowds rushed to make space. He tried to decide what to do. He was too happy to fight. The girl was pulled away from him. He turned to his attacker – a lanky man, his features tight with anger – and lifted his open hands, petting lightly at the man's chest like a kitten. Just before he was scooped off his feet by bouncers, Milo laughed at the confusion he'd inflicted. He was carried out almost horizontally and to his surprise was not thrown but placed down gently. When he got his bearings, he found himself alone on the pavement with the doorman who had first let him in.

"You didn't last long."

"There's no justice in the world," said Milo. "They're good though." He gestured to the doorway where the other bouncers had gone. "Had me out in a few seconds – put me down nice and softly too."

"I hired them, they ought to be good." Milo started walking. "Don't come back here."

"What? … Ever?"

"Ever."

"So this is goodbye, then? I hate goodbyes, haha!" He spun around, gave a salute and made his way into the night.

A few minutes later he was sauntering aimlessly when he saw her. The same strapless blue dress and wavy hair. He couldn't believe his luck and yelled out to her from the opposite pavement. She froze in surprise. As he crossed over Milo saw that she was a different woman.

"It's ok, don't be shocked. I thought you were someone else." He mimicked her cat-in-headlights expression and she smiled and began walking – slowly, like an invitation to him.

"Is anywhere else open?" he asked. Her lips pouted. They were damp and springy and distracted him so much he nearly walked into a lamppost. "Fuck!" He dodged. "Haha! That was your fault."

"How was it my fault?"

"You're distracting … I'm going on this side." He crossed her path away from the road. Her dress had ridden halfway down her breasts. Her heels clipped on the pavement in time with his feet. "I like it when I see a couple with legs moving at the same time," he said, admiring the line of her cheekbones and a small gap in her front teeth that he was so fond of in women. "Like they're a sort of creature with four legs."

"Romantic of you."

"I'm a romantic dude."

She wobbled, leaning into him briefly. The bars were all closed. Behind them a group argued loudly about taxi fares.

"Where are your friends?"

"They fucked off," she said testily.

Milo grinned inwardly with gratitude. "I'll be your friend," he said and put his arm around her for a moment.

"Thanks, Romantic Dude." Her words were fluid and playful.

"My name's Milo."

It would be temporary, but just then he loved her. He loved her mellow speech and springy lips. And he loved the trust she had in him.

"Are you following me home, Milo?" she asked as they turned a corner onto a quieter road. Her mascara was smudged and the powder of foundation showed up around her nostrils when they passed a street light.

"You're supposed to tell me your name."

"You don't *care*, Milo."

They had slowed and now he stopped and turned to her, weakened. When he held her cheek and kissed her it was only for comfort. He touched the curve of her spine, tingling like it was his first kiss, or his last. When their heads parted she wiped his cheek with her thumb.

"You're crying," she said under her breath. Then kissed him harder, digging her nails into the back of his neck.

17

Disappear

SHE WASN'T SNORING, just breathing unevenly with a whistle on the inhale. It was keeping Milo awake. The bed was too small for two. She'd moved over to the far edge but still he could feel the heat radiating from her body. On the floor their clothes were mixed together. Her bra sat across the crumbs of his empty sandwich packet. A car alarm whined somewhere in the distance and the curtain swayed by the open window. He lay with one leg and half his stomach under the duvet, not bothering to try and sleep. With every whistle his discomfort increased until the side of his body next to her crawled with repulsion. She lay on her side with forearms crossed, her mouth half-open, makeup smudged into the pillow. "Disssss," he murmured. The 'S's whistled like a reply to her. "Disappear." A spell, he cast it only with the vaguest hope.

He longed for that cool stability of being alone. His head and face were beginning to ache and his mouth still had the fruity twang leftover from the night. With the gin worn off she was still as beautiful. Their brief story replayed now in the most clownish way. He'd cried as he kissed her, what better way to melt her heart and yet they were genuine tears, springing from the same void that made all the others love him. Poor Milo. He chuckled dryly.

"Dis-appear…" He wriggled his foot, kicking an empty condom packet onto the floor. "It's romantic, disappearance." Her chest sank slowly and rose. He looked at her breasts pressed together, the bumpy brown outline of her nipples, her neck pink from his teeth. *Disappear together.* Someone said that to me, I can't remember who." He waited for another whistle, then continued. "But who disappears *together*? If you can see each other then you're not gone, you're still somewhere… Too many riddles." His words were breaking half way above a whisper. "As for you… Can you feel that I want you gone?" She stirred, moved her arm and groaned cosily. "I get that feeling every so often, that something wants me gone. Something that used to love me back when I was new." He edged close enough to feel her breaths on his face and was about to speak again, but instead just waited then rolled carefully back to his pillow. A car rumbled past. "Disappear together ... HA!" he said louder, suddenly remembering where he'd heard that phrase.

In the bathroom, he turned on the tap and bent over to drink from it. His jeans and shirt were crumpled together on the same piece of carpet. He put them on, not bothering with shoes. A few rooms down he saw their light was on. A bit early perhaps, but they'd forgive him. He knocked. Isa opened the door cautiously, blocking the view of the room with his body. He brightened when he recognised Milo.

"We had heard there was someone here who *knew* us." He shook Milo's hand emphatically.

"How much do they know?" said Baby with a snigger.

"I know it's late. Or early ..."

"It's ok. We don't have normal bedtimes." Isa led him to where the duvet and pillows had been laid out on the floor and Baby sat cross legged, stirring the liquid in a plastic bowl. Both of them had the look of wired exhaustion Milo knew well.

"I've never seen so much in one place," said Milo, taking extra care as he climbed past the bowl and onto a free pillow.

"I know, I'm scared I'm going to spill it. I'm stirring so softly."

Isa dumped himself between them.

"Where have you two been?"

"Need you ask?"

"I guess not."

"And you, Milo?"

"I'm disappearing. For a while."

"Oh, we know all about that. Don't we, Baby?" He offered Milo a spoonful. It glinted white and rippled with the shaking of his arm.

"How much do you want for it?"

"Don't be a fool. Drink up. And be merry."

"He doesn't seem merry."

"He doesn't, does he Baby? I think he came to our room to be cheered up."

Milo swallowed from the spoon and the glass of water that followed, feeling like a child taking his medicine. They small-talked while he waited for the high. Mainly about the Hospital; they had little else in common. This kept them going till the symptoms came. This time there was no deluge of happiness, just a quiet gratitude. Isa nodded knowingly, seeing their guest gradually join their level.

Baby spoke weakly. "Look at us, in our circle. We should be telling ghost stories."

"Once upon a time…" Isa began, "a man and a woman were sitting together in the dead of night, when they heard a knock at the door…"

"And it was Milo," Baby interrupted.

"Fuck, you ruined the joke." He gave her a gentle push and she toppled onto her back with a groan and lay there. "That's the end of her. Do you know any, Milo?"

Baby chortled to herself. Milo had been locked in position, rapidly descending further than he'd ever gone. He tried to answer but couldn't.

Isa looked equally smitten. "Strong, ah?"

Milo was sweating. As he tried again to respond, a line of saliva ran from his lip.

"Let me ask you, Milo – do you know what tiptoe is?" Baby had passed out. Isa hunched over the bowl, dipping the spoon up and down. "People call it a drug. It's not a drug." Milo wrenched himself from the trance long enough to notice a movement out the window, like a fly bouncing against the glass. "Do you believe in witches?" Milo swooned and wiped the saliva from his chin. "Tiptoe's not a drug, it's a spell." His heart rate was alarming him. In an effort to ease it he wobbled to his feet. "Getting the shakes? I thought you were stronger, haha. I never see you sober, after all. Mind you, I won't be trying to stand anytime soon."

Milo propped himself up on the wall and threw the window open, gasping the clean air. Behind him he heard the slurping sound of Isa taking another hit. The base of the sky glowed with the first hints of morning. The city was as still as he'd ever seen it – no cars moving, no people, just concrete and watery glass stretching away.

"I thought you two were disappearing together," he asked once he was steady enough to speak.

"We're working on it."

The next time Milo looked around Isa was slouched forward with his eyes closed, about to collapse next to Baby. Feeling like the only person left awake in the world, Milo surveyed the last of the night. At the edge of the window, almost out of range, he saw the movement again. It was not a fly but something larger, far in the distance, rising and falling, with wings as grey as the concrete.

18

Homely

MILO DIDN'T KISS HER when he returned. Not even a mechanical married-man kiss. His hair had grown longer and was beginning to curl. Only Ivy had known his hair was curly; now the whole world did. His cheek was bruised and his t-shirt crossed with lines of mud.

"I need a shower," was all he said as he walked past her up the stairs.

The water heater hummed. She stood below it trying not to pace. *Chain-smoking tramp* or *chain smoker*? She still hadn't decided. Nearly half an hour later the humming stopped and he came back down the stairs dressed in a pair of ripped jeans and a dressing gown. They waited opposite each other at the kitchen table, both knowing what was about to happen. She had practised different versions of this scene, from the quiet regret to the furniture smashing and every other type of goodbye. Milo sat bolt-upright focused on her, dressing gown half open revealing a scratch mark across his chest and nipple. He was about to speak but she jumped in.

"I can't do this anymore. You know that, don't you?"

"Yea. I know that."

"I look for excuses to forgive you. Maybe you're younger than me, and you married too early. Maybe you're insecure. You love me really, you're just lost."

He listened, perfectly still, arms draped across the edges of the chair. He looked like some heartthrob for lonely teenagers, with his stubble and that drunken dampness in his eyes. "This time, while you've been gone I've tried to think about this objectively. And it's hard to do. The first few days I just pushed you out of my mind as much as I could; after that I felt the excuses coming back. But I looked closely at these excuses, and the way I made them. I noticed that I scrabble around for them in the most desperate way. In that time between you hurting me and when I think of a reason why it's ok, I'm like some chain smoker scrounging cigarette butts off the floor.

I want to forgive you so badly, Milo." She made sure her voice was steady. "But I don't I love you. You're just a habit that I can't drop." She tried to mimic the nonchalant style he used occasionally.

He absorbed what she said wearily and then spoke at last. "Did you practise that speech when I was in the shower…? I was trying to think of a speech too. But I haven't been able to come up with anything… People always told me I'd lose you, but I don't like following advice, even when it's good." This was all he had.

"What is it that you *want*, Milo?"

"I don't know. I don't think about that stuff."

"You just do things."

"Just… that."

"Why did you marry me?"

His eyes left her. "You're homely."

She wanted to be angry, but all she felt was a peculiar dread.

"Homely? What do you mean homely?"

"I mean, you're my home. But I'm restless."

"You want excitement, then to come back to me when you're all drained out."

"Yes."

She realised it then: at some point, whether days ago or just this evening stood under the shower, he had made a commitment to absolute honesty. He was answering without resistance, watching the revelations wound her, knowing she couldn't resist going deeper.

"How many women have you slept with since we got married?"

"Eight." He said it without hesitation, but his voice had changed. Perhaps he had a lump in his throat.

Ivy continued defiantly. "And how many since we were first dating?"

He sprung to his feet and went to the corner of the room. "Eleven."

"Just three before? Were you less adventurous back then?"

He hoisted himself up on two worktop ledges and hung there suspended a few inches above the floor. "How about you?"

"One."

"One as in me?"

"No, one apart from you."

He nodded at the floor, still propped up by the strength of his arms. When he thumped back down she stood up. Just in front of him, she felt a force field push her back and realised she would never be able to touch him again. She had wanted to run her finger along the scratch mark; it seemed right that the skin above his heart should sting.

"It was Aaron."

Milo nodded again, resigned to his fate.

"When?"

Studying his minute reactions, Ivy told the story step by step, adding in every detail she could remember. She told him about the day her exams ended. This new chapter of life suddenly open. The beers that couldn't cure her nerves when she looked at him. New nerves she'd never felt before. Everyone asking *what did you write for question seven?* Everyone but the two of them. The fascination he had for her that no one else did. The piles of autumn leaves.

"And the rest is history," Milo cut in.

"I was going to tell you the intimate details. I hope you're not getting jealous."

"A bit."

"Do you want to know if he was better than you?"

"Not really."

"Or what people said to us when we came home with bits of leaves in our hair and clothes? You see, it sounds very sweet the way I'm describing it. But it wasn't sweet." She leaned in closer. "It was filthy. And it got filthier every time I met him. "

"Aaron, eh?" Milo forced out a laugh.

"Even before I knew you cheated and before I had any reason to, I've wanted to crush something in you, Milo. That smugness you have, it irritates the fuck out of me. I'm quite spiteful, have you noticed? You've never noticed much about me. It's funny really, if you knew how rotten I am maybe you'd never have got bored of me."

Milo rubbed his hair. "Maybe."

"Sleep in there," she pointed to the living room, "but please don't be here when I get home tomorrow. We'll sort the paperwork once you're gone." As she'd been speaking, the dread had grown making her nauseous. She'd delivered every sentence as planned but what an anti-climax it was. His hurt was hidden as usual, she should have known.

"I'll leave tonight. All I needed was a shower."

19

Too late for her

IT WAS NEARLY NOON when he was ready to leave. He decided to wait until the second hand clicked into place. In the street Roan passed a man he slightly recognised but neither said hello. The sun was toasting the back of his neck; he suspected he might get burnt but decided not to go back. At the same moment he realised he had been wearing the same T-shirt for over a week and it was dotted with food stains. He had no destination in mind and kept going vaguely toward the city limits. He came to a street of detached houses, many boarded up. A discarded sofa stripped of its cushions blocked one porch. Another front path was breaking apart as roots forced their way up. The trees lining either side of the road were shedding their leaves and every so often he kicked through the piles in his way.

Once, as a child, he was ringing door bells with his school friends and running away. One door opened only seconds later – he had turned and sprinted for so many blocks he lost count. When he stopped he was desperate for air. In the middle of one breath a fly darted into his throat making him vomit profusely onto the pavement. This memory had been lost until now.

He heard a smash from inside a house and a woman shouting. Roan stopped. There was a man as well, trying to calm her. He edged towards the front gate, curious but tilting ready to walk on in a casual escape. The man said something, *Believe* maybe. There was another smash, louder than the first. Roan clutched the gate. The front garden was overgrown like others in the street, with dandelions sprouting up through tangles of long grass. The argument moved further out of range. Roan was about to continue on his way when the downstairs curtains were flung open. Instinctively he ducked under the wall, sure he had been spotted. Should he crawl away? Or should he wait as he was now, expecting someone to loom over him from the other side? To his relief the argument continued.

Roan swivelled round so he was sitting on the pavement, knees bent, looking either way along a clear road. They didn't sound young; their voices had past arguments in them. The woman spoke again, more softly. He gripped his knees tightly. It was not so much fear that kept him from moving but a fascination with his own mischief. Should he peep over the wall? They were engrossed now, he was safe. Half way through turning he stopped. There were houses on the opposite street that he had not considered: the neighbours could be watching him. The shutters were closed on one house; the other was partially blocked by trees. He scanned them and, seeing no one, knelt below the wall just too low to see. There was moss clinging to the bricks. He moved up slowly till he was peering through the uppermost bristles of moss. There was a dining room, a table partly disguised by a net curtain with a man and woman beside it, hidden from the hips down. For a moment he crouched with legs half unfolded, then stood up fully.

A siren in the distance, it was getting louder. At the window the shadows changed. He recognised the shape of a face behind the net curtain. It was looking at him. Roan stumbled into a sprint. The beat of his feet on the pavement thumped out the siren. Only when he had cleared the street and turned three corners did he stop, wheezing heavily through his nose. The siren was growing fainter. It took him a long time to stop shaking.

As he began walking again, the face was still imprinted faintly on his vision. Guilt kept his body stiff and pointing forward, as though one irregular step would announce his crimes. He tried to shake it off but it only sunk deeper, rotting away inside him. The streets here were the same – detached, boxy houses with grey brick finishing. Roan gave them a wide berth, staying by the road in case they lashed out. The sunlight flashed in and out of range through the branches of the roadside trees.

"Why should I feel guilty?" he asked himself aloud, checking around in case anyone should hear. "I'm the nicest person I know." As he said this his shadow stretched ahead of him, momentarily visible – lumbering and monstrous. Kindness was comical in a man of his size. A fluttery heart in his gigantic frame. The shadow merged with the dappled shade on the next pavement.

In a window a blind snapped open revealing an elderly woman among the stalks of indoor plants. She stared past Roan at the road and the parked cars. She reminded him of Ms Limms; the exact sourness she would grow into in thirty years. And the plants too. He stayed by the driveway, watching once again. The woman did not seem to notice him and there was no wall to duck under if she did. The driveway was open and he stood in the middle, as conspicuous as could be. The other windows of the house were all blocked by curtains, yellowed by years of sunlight. The front door was large and foreboding with the kind of gargoyle knocker he had only seen in dated horror films.

Roan held his ground. Why should he feel guilty for wanting to watch? The woman craned forwards, her nose almost touching the glass. What was she searching for? Or whom? A quick inspection showed no-one approaching on either side. He took a tentative step forward. The woman's white hair trailed in strands down to her cheek bones. From just a few steps away, Roan saw the milky blue of her irises – perhaps she was blind. Her lumpy arthritic hands hung like talons. He saw her bemusement, crossed with that concern so profound only old people understand it. He felt like her protector. With a proud flexing of his shoulders he took another step forward into her driveway. As he did her eyes locked onto his as though he were suddenly no longer invisible. A few feet from each other, separated by the glass, they both waited, Roan struggling to show his benevolence. Within this deadlock every sound was extra sharp; the scrunching of his soles on the concrete, faraway bird calls. To think she wouldn't hear them, locked behind the glass, a permanent stranger. Cloud was gathering overhead. He pictured carrying her frail body. *Don't be concerned anymore.* But she would stay as she was. It was too late for her. This was Roan's last thought as he left the driveway, her bemused gaze following him all the way down the road.

20

Mr C. Breeze

"HELLO, COULD I SPEAK TO Mrs Goro-sha-bia-lendo, please?"
"Mrs Goralesco?"
"Yes."
"Yes?"
"Good afternoon, I'm Milo. I'm calling on behalf of ..."
"Mrs Goralesco here."
"... Thomson Optical. You put your name on our website."
"No, no more." The phone went dead.

That night Milo had slept on the back seat of his car, curled in a ball with a jacket over his head to block out the sunrise. His shift began at one in the afternoon. Until the last moment he had lain there with the bustle of the day around him, forcing himself to back to sleep. His seat in the office had been left empty. As he waited for the next call, he dragged the curser of the mouse from side to side, moving the displays around idly.

Next to him, his neighbour was doing the same. "I swear to God, Milo, I can't deal with one more day in this place. I should be doing so much more than this, Milo. I shouldn't be taking half hour lunch breaks and drinking that shitty coffee." It was a familiar conversation. Milo had never felt trapped in the way others were. He had no children, no real commitments; he could always drop his headset on the desk and be forgotten. "I mean, I went upstairs to get a leavers' form. I asked the big woman where I could find the leavers' forms. She didn't even look up, just said *Over by the sale sheets.* They don't care about you here. We're farm animals to them."

"They don't kill us though. They usually kill farm animals."

"They're killing me softly, Milo, I swear to God."

"You're leaving then?"

"I am. I've got the form. I just need to do some job hunting. There's never any time to search for jobs at this place, I mean, once you get home and make your dinner and—*Good day there, can I speak to Mr Liezel?"*

Milo filled in the outcome for his last call: *Call back customer in … twenty five minutes?* Yes, twenty five – long enough to get settled. The next call came through immediately. It was an answer phone; he muted his headset and waited for the machine to play out. *I'm sorry I didn't hear anything; please leave your message after the tone.*

A scrunched up piece of paper bounced over the desk and into his lap. Aaron was waving at him from a few desks away. They had not noticed each other till now. Milo nodded and pointed at the clock.

"The thing is, Milo. If you were running a business, would you treat people like this? I mean, when I had my business I made a few mistakes but I made sure I treated my staff right."

Two minutes until break, the next call came in. "Hello!?" barked a busy-sounding man.

"*… Hello,*" replied Milo, as slowly as he could.

"Well?"

"*Hello there.*"

"Yes? Out with it!"

"*Mr Graves?*"

"I am."

"*Is that Mr Graves?*" Milo leaned onto his arm, assuming his favourite angle of repose. He was sure he could string this out for two minutes.

"Damn it, man. Who are you?"

"*Easy there.*"

"Well what do you want, who are you? I'm Mr Graves, now who are you?"

"*Milo.*"

"From?"

Milo left as long a pause as he could muster. "*I'm calling on behalf of* Thomson Optical.*"*

"What do you want with me?"

"*I'm glad that you asked that.*"

"What?"

"So how is Friday for you? For your consultation, I'm putting you down for three o'clock. Do you have your credit card there?"

"I *beg* your pardon?"

"Are you still there?"

"What is the meaning of this?"

"Meaning of what?"

"In the name of ..." Mr Graves left the line and for the last minute Milo put on his jacket and poised for departure.

Clumped together with the other smokers, Aaron and Milo stood by the wall, watching the brushes spin at the carwash across the road.

"So how did it happen?" Aaron asked.

"I just told you."

"I know but ... Was it sad, you know? You seem quite relaxed about the whole thing."

"It was sad."

"Of course. I mean, you're getting a divorce, that's bound to be hard."

"Is it?"

"Not that I'd know. But of course it's going to be tough. I'm here."

"Where?"

Aaron looked confused, Milo laughed. "Sorry, I've been asking these dumb questions to people all morning. It's quite fun. I recommend it."

"Oh ... Recommend what?"

"Haha, yea like that."

Aaron blew the ash from the end of his cigarette. "Milo, I have to get out of here soon."

"You too?"

"Yea, too much man. Too much repetition."

"Go then."

"I will. I'll take a leaf out of your book and disappear ... Ivy was worried, you know."

"Sure."

"What are you going to do now? You can stay at mine if you want."

Milo scraped the sole of his foot slowly down the wall. "I doubt I'll do that. Not that I hold grudges."

"Grudges for what?" Aaron passed his cigarette from one hand to another.

"Ivy spoke to me."

"She spoke to you?"

"Yes."

The brushes across the road stopped and drooped to half their size. Aaron cleared his throat, preparing for a *Sorry*.

When the next call came through it was another impatient woman, probably middle aged, probably in the middle of eating an elaborate lunch cooked to say *I still love you even though you're fat and impatient*. He listened to the *Hellos*, then hung up. The side of his cheek ached; the bruise was fading to yellow. By his feet was a bag with a set of clothes and toiletries, enough to last him the next few days. Ivy had the rest of his things. She wouldn't throw them out, though she might have liked to. At worst, she would use his favourite shirt as a duster; even then she would probably put it in the wash for him.

The next call was an answer machine, the one after that was a fax tone. On one fortunate day he had gone a whole two hours getting nothing but answer phones, just by luck. An incredible coincidence squandered on such a feeble cause. His neighbour was deep into a call, pointing into the desk at the end of each sentence. Management had told him to get a sale a day for the rest of the week if he was to keep his job. Listening to the whirring of another fax tone, Milo studied him. His tie was trailing low onto his groin; he looked like some forgotten school boy.

Milo's earpiece bleeped again. "Hello?"

"*Hello, can I speak to Miss Alice Reeves?*"

"Nope."

The next call came with no gap. "Hello?"

"*Can I speak to Mr C. Breeze?*"

"That's me."

"*It's Milo. Do you fancy a consultation?*"

"Oh yes, is that Thomson Optical? I was speaking to someone about you. Do you think you could organise a consultation for me, if you don't mind?" He was jovial. Milo pictured an elderly man with glasses hung around his neck by a string, a twinkle and all day to talk. There was no game to play with friendly people. Talking to them was all too linear and predictable. "Milo, is it?"

Milo waited. *"How does it feel to be named after a wind?"* he asked at last.

"... There's a wind called Charlie?"

"No I mean, C. Breeze. As in a breeze by the sea."

"Goodness me, you know I never thought of that."

"Really?"

"Never thought to interpret it like that."

"Really?"

"Hahaha! I'm not that dim. Tell me, what are you named after?"

"I've no idea."

"What's you're second name?"

"Blakely."

"You sound glum, Milo?"

A sympathetic ear, an invisible friend. He weighed up two choices. "Bear with me a second, I'm going to put you on hold." He stood up, peeled off the headset and slung his bag over one shoulder.

21

Here of all places

CLOUD SQUASHED LOW OVER THE CITY. Milo removed his tie with the ceremonious ripping motion he had always imagined. He looped it over the branch of a tree and carefully retied the knot. For the past months he had worked at this same building, leant in his favourite position on his same seat, saying similar words. It was all quite hypnotic. Walking on, he wondered if he would see the tie again and if so how wrinkled the rain and lost time would have made it. *If I see that tie again, Milo pondered… Then what? What should the stake be? If I see the tie again, I'll buy myself a double whisky and drink it sitting on the bank of the river.* That seemed quite a tame idea but a pleasant one. So pleasant in fact that… yes – it still fluttered from a branch. Whisky it is.

The landlord yelled after him not to take his glass outside. He crossed the road. A van beeped and screeched to a halt beside him. Milo hadn't noticed it approach or even thought to look. Behind the windscreen he saw flailing arms and heard muffled curses. He chuckled and stopped, taking time to enjoy the tickle of alcohol in his throat. The van revved at him aggressively. He waited, smiling at the driver who was hidden by the reflection of clouds. Cars were clogging up behind. A couple of different horns sounded. Another sip of whisky and another smile to the angry windscreen. He experimented with different smiles he had never tried: a movie star smile, a shop assistant smile, an axe murderer smile. The window of the van rolled down and a haggard man with a gold tooth stuck his head out.

"GET OUT THE ROAD, YOU DOG'S DICK!"

The warmth of the whisky and the smiles kept him safe. Another sip and then, with a jovial wave, he took one step to the side and stopped again. The van jerked forward and braked. More insults, more beeps. If the man got out of the van and attacked him, who would overpower who? What then would he do with a knocked-out driver and an empty van with keys in the ignition? Just as the possibilities began to excite him the van backed up, mounted the pavement and swerved past him. A shot of saliva pinged by his ear. Milo made his way to the other side of the road giving another wave to the departing van, hoping his gold-toothed friend would see him in the wing mirror. The wave was the kind a politician gives voters, both jovial and robotic.

At the side of the road he stepped onto the walkway by the river, listening to the last few curses as the backed-up cars drove away. With an action as simple as stopping in the wrong place he had generated such hatred. He marvelled at the absurdity and beauty of it. The wall next to him bordered the river. Before turning toward it, he placed another bet: *If the tide is in, I'll jump in and swim; if the tide is out, I'll sit and drink my drink in peace.* He rather regretted this, it was not a warm day and he had nowhere to shower and change if he needed to. To his relief he saw marsh and debris and a trickle of river. He hoisted himself over till he was sitting with feet dangling high over empty space. Of all the people he knew there was not one he wanted to call and ask for shelter. This was partly pride but more just a general sickness with people and their kindness.

The seagulls here were bigger than he remembered them to be. They swooped below him over the scatters of rock and litter, like fearsome birds of prey. He scrabbled around for a stone to throw at them but found only smooth concrete. His pockets were empty, but for the essentials. All he had was the glass, which still had a full measure left in it. The temptation was too strong; he swigged the whole lot and hurled the glass at the nearest bird. He caught it dead-on, sending the creature tumbling backward. Milo laughed so hard he nearly overbalanced and fell off the ledge.

If he fell he would not die, it wasn't quite that high. He could break a leg though. If he were confined to a wheel chair that day, Ivy would probably take pity on him and wheel him around. She could never resist the lure of a good deed, despite everything she said. If he were sprawled out on the rubble below, legs and spine broken, he wondered if he would call for help. Or just wait patiently for the river to carry him away. Maybe cowardice would strike before the tide came in.

Orange sunlight cut through from the far bank. Evening was coming. He thought about the last few days he had spent tiptoed and happy. Just a sour white liquid in a vial could fill you with crippling joy. Chemicals reacting. Even happiness for a normal man is a chemical reaction. When he gets his dick sucked or watches a sunset one test tube is poured into another. Someone walks out in front of his van; mix in a different poison.

His car was parked a few blocks down. When he reached it he searched through the glove compartment and the boot and under the seats until he found them: wrapped up in plastic and sticky tape, vials of familiar liquid set aside for this sort of day. He turned the music as loud as it would go and headed for the main road, savouring the bitter taste one more time. The drive was aimless. He didn't read the road signs. On straight stretches of highway he focused in on one single point ahead, daring himself to close his eyes for one second. Then two. Then three. Somewhere in the wasteland at the edge of the city there was a movement – some strange animal, or just a trick of dust. The drive came to an end when he recognised a square on the horizon growing into a building.

"How did I end up here of all places?" He stepped out and looked up at the empty window frames and the flaking brickwork.

Tufts of dry weeds poked through the dust below him. Milo scraped his feet as he walked, making little clouds waft up around his ankles. It seemed frailer today; the sun showed all the hidden erosion. He approached the black square, the open mouth where the double doors had been.

Inside, the hallways resounded with the sound of clinking glass as he kicked empty bottles out his way. Above him hung a line of fluorescent light tubes, long ago extinguished. The fittings were filled with dust and clusters of small bugs, barely visible in the gloom. The walls were dented and disguised under years of graffiti. He peered into each door he passed, trying to navigate from memory. Some of the smaller rooms were cluttered with items of furniture – garden benches with planks missing, rotting sofa beds – all covered in dirt and dwarfed by the high ceilings. At the end of the corridor the space opened up, dividing into more passageways and a flight of stairs.

"HELLO!" he shouted, testing the echoes. While he stood wondering which way to take, he tasted the bitter remnants in his throat. Not long now. Would there be another rave that night? Was he their first and most eager guest, or would he gurn his night away alone on a mouldy mattress? He skipped up the stairs, calling another *Hello* and a howl. The metal creaked as he climbed. A whole section of wall in the upstairs corridor had fallen, allowing the sunlight to break through from the adjacent room. Some of the doors remained intact. One had been detached from its hinges and leant across the opening, revealing the floorboards and walls inside consumed by ivy.

The first hints of tiptoe crept in. His stomach was empty, so it wouldn't be long in taking hold. He pushed the next door open, seeing a nest of pigeons and floors caked in excrement. The next had a hole where the floorboards had rotted and fallen through. A head-rush sent him reeling. It was coming faster than expected. All he needed was a bit of space. There was a spluttering sound; perhaps it came from him. He stumbled into the next room and crouched down, his body convulsing. When he blinked the inside of his eyelids were white. Just before sinking he remembered his wedding ring – he had forgotten to remove it.

22

Animal

"WHY DO I END UP HERE of all places?" Roan muttered, listening to the pelting rain outside. "Why do you end up here, Roan?" He sat cross-legged on the hard wooden floor, clothes soaked to the skin. A deep loneliness filled him. "I have animal instincts…" He needed to talk continuously; the lulls were too eerie. "Why didn't your instincts stop you falling over in that hole?" He stroked the grazes on his knees, wondering how much blood the darkness hid from him. It felt unnatural but he spoke aloud again. "Animal! AN … EEE … MAL. Mall … ani-mall. UNIMUL!" This was all he could think to say for a while. The repetition was like a spell. The thought of animals being drawn to him through the dark disturbed him more than it amused. "I might be treated in here one day. They might restore it. HA! Doctor, I was here one night in the dark, before it was a hospital again. I sat and shouted *Animal* at the shadows. Shivering my FUCKING ASS OFF!" A draught ran through his wet clothes, whistling past his bones. "I'm a fucking frozen skeleton. FUCK! FUCK! FUCK! FUCK!" He sniggered to himself as he imagined telling someone how he had reached this place and the condition he'd travelled in. "Doctor, I went for a walk one day. When I was bored and younger. I walked around the city limits, through the grass, till my socks were wet and my knees were aching, till I was lost. Till I was FUCKING lost." When he was older he could swear as much as he wanted. "But The Hospital sucked me in. I saw its big ugly crumbling face in the rain. It sucked me in for company. Or it sucked me in just to suck me in and eat me up … Back then I wasn't quite the distinguished old cunt you know me as. I wasn't quite as happy as I am. I wasn't quite … HA!" He sounded like the sum of all the most absurd characters he had ever played. Shivers ran through him uncontrollably. He decided to stand up and move around. When he did, his legs almost gave way. He continued to mumble, giving up on real words, just making noises. Somewhere the moon had slithered out from the rainclouds.

At first he took it as a trick of his light-starved eyes. The outline was too faint. Something angular moving across the floor. Too slow and deliberate to be blown by a draught. It made a clipping sound as it approached. Roan stood still. It was no taller than his knees. He squinted just enough to see a jagged body. It stopped in front of him, contorted itself upright and let out a dry rustle of breath. When it spoke, its voice was almost human.

The walls are grafittied it said. *Do you want to see?*

Roan flung himself back as a surge of flame came between them, illuminating the room for half a second and plunging them back into deeper darkness. The walls were layered with black writing.

Did you see it? What if I said it was all done by the same person?

"What person?" The cold subsided, perhaps it was the shock.

Do you listen when you walk? There's a crunching. It's infested.

Roan had only heard the rain. Something tickled the skin under his shirt, then above his sock. He shook them off vigorously.

They won't harm you. Another draught passed through. *You're shaking.*

"I'm cold."

How many layers of skin do you have?

"How the fuck should I know?"

Do you want another one? If I give you one, you can never take it off.

"You're a creep."

Sometimes, when no-one is here, I've no need to creep at all.

Another tickle ran up Roan's arm. He wriggled. "Can you get them off me?"

It's infested. I told you. Don't mind them, they're too stupid to harm you; for all they know you're their queen.

"You're more of a bug than me. At least I walk on two legs like a human."

It's dark in here, Roan. And there's no-one to see who's human and who's not.

"I should photograph you. And give the picture to the zoo. They'll come after you and take you to a lab." Roan grinned, stretching his chapped lips.

This is the lab and you came all the way here. But what kind of genius could cure you? It scuttled up closer.

"Stop breathing on my leg. It's disgusting." Roan lumbered backward again; the ground was sticky, like he was crunching over popcorn.

There's breath on your leg. Do you need the leg doctor or the lung doctor?

"I need an exorcist."

You're an artist aren't you?

"So?"

Your demons make everything beautiful.

"*You're* not very beautiful."

Its neck bent back to study him. *But you can't see me. I ought to turn the lights on.*

Before Roan could reply, the room was illuminated and intensely white. He found himself lying on his side, ribs aching and stiff. The sun shone straight through onto his curled-up body. The air was warmer now and his clothes were dry. From the corridor came the sound of radio static and many footsteps. He clambered to his knees and she was there.

"Stay where you are!" she said. Was it her?

23

He's a beast

WHEN THE RINGS RAN OUT, Ivy put down the receiver a little too loudly.

"Are you doing what I think you're doing?" Ruth called from the next room.

"No. Whatever that is." She re-entered to see her sister sitting at the mirror, half made-up, looking exasperated.

"You're calling Milo! She's calling Milo! Tell her!" They were in Ivy's living room, preparing for the wedding. Their parents sat next to each other on a sofa, looking stiff in their formal dress. Ruth pursed her lips in the mirror and beamed at the make-up artist who crouched beside her, lining up his brushes. No-one responded to her objections, beyond a non-committal "ah well" from their father. Ivy had her bridesmaid dress laid out on the upstairs bed, waiting for the other women to arrive before she put it on. Their parents had been dressed up since waking.

"I wasn't calling Milo. Just… concentrate on you, will you?"

"Concentration!" she said into the mirror as her cheeks were blushed. "My sister's getting divorced," she told the make-up artist, who replied with a sympathetic hum.

"The circle of life, eh?" put in their father. Next to him, their mother scoffed at his philosophical tone.

"It's ok. He was an idiot," Ruth went on. "She thinks I don't know she's trying to call him. It won't make it easier you know." Ivy smiled at her father, who was making talking motions with his hand. "It's tough to break up with someone after so long, but you have to realise…"

"Ruth darling, shut up will you," their mother interrupted. "You don't know what you're talking about."

"Easy tiger…Mum."

"Tiger-mum. Huhuhu!" their father chuckled.

"Back in your box, Henry." Their mother was a tall, elegant woman with smooth white hair and a mock-solemn expression, like a parody headmistress. Their father was podgy and gleamed with private jokes.

"Divorces are tough," said the make-up artist in a quiet moment.

"Have you been through one?" Ruth asked.

"Me? No."

Ivy went to sit on the arm of the sofa next to her father who patted her knee jauntily.

"I'm getting married."

"You must be excited," the makeup artist said absently.

"Who knows what I am."

Ivy viewed them all, contented, enjoying her parents' presence and the lack of scrutiny on her.

"I can glue that up while I'm here." Henry pointed to the coffee table, which had one leg askew.

"If it makes you happy, Dad."

"You're HOT, that's what you are," said the makeup artist. Her father put his arm around Ivy, gazing at the table with a faraway tearful expression. "Don't cry, it's only a table," the makeup artist winked over at their sofa. Ruth cackled loudly.

Taking advantage of the brief distraction, Ivy went back to the kitchen and pressed redial. She had lost count of her tries and expected no answer. She hadn't even bothered to close the door.

Ruth yelled through to her. "Are you at it again in there? … Hello, talk to me!"

"Hello?" It was a woman.

"My name's Ivy Blakely, I'm from the school."

"Oh?"

"Carne's school."

"I see."

"Who am I speaking to, please?" She crossed over and closed the door with her foot.

"Ivy is it? Ms Limms."

"I've spoken to Mr Hansel before…"

"Mr Hansel, yes."

"Is he home?"

"He's not home. No."

"It's quite important I speak to him. Carne's been missing from school and we haven't been able to reach anyone."

"Have the police been informed?"

Ivy cleared her throat. "No ... So you haven't seen Carne this week either?"

"I don't believe that's what I said."

"I'm sorry, have you or haven't you?"

"Excuse me?"

Ivy hesitated, unsure whether she ought to be angry. "When can I speak to Mr Hansel?"

"If you give me your details, I'll ensure he gets in touch."

Ivy tapped her teeth together, fidgeting with the phone cord. "It's important. Carne could be in danger."

"What on earth makes you think that?"

"I haven't seen Carne for a week. He's missed five days of school."

"I'll inform Mr Hansel of your concerns."

"When can I speak to him, please?"

"I'll get him to call you as soon as he's free to speak."

"I'm sorry to be intrusive," Ivy probed, trying to disguise her impatience, "but can I ask you whether or not you have seen Carne this last week?"

Ms Limms sighed and responded more amiably. "Carne is safe. But it's not my place to explain any further."

"Right." From the other room she heard Ruth shrieking with laughter.

"Favourite of yours is he?" Ms Limms asked.

"Unofficially, yes."

"He'd be mine too. Beautiful and strange."

"May I ask what relation you are to Peter?"

"Admirable. That you're going beyond the call of duty for this boy."

"It's entirely my duty."

"He talked about you ..." Ms Limms trailed off. Someone else was in the background of the call, a man. Ivy strained to hear, blocking the mirth in the next room.

"Are you hiding me, Ms Limms?" It was Peter Hansel.

"I thought you should be left in peace."

"Odd choice of word." There was a bustle of indistinguishable sounds. She heard his mouth by the phone before he spoke. "My secretary of ten years – she knows me better than I know myself."

"Oh."

"So you want to know why the boy's left you without saying goodbye."

"I'd like to know when he'll be back."

"He's not well."

"I'm sorry to hear it. What's wrong with him?"

"He has mysterious disease. Don't you agree?"

"What mysterious disease?"

"Mysterious disease. He hides. He has secrets. Little boys shouldn't have secrets. What do you think? Almost like he's not a boy at all." He spoke with a strange wistfulness.

"I've noticed how unhappy he is at school. He's a puzzle."

"What drives you, Mrs Blakely?"

"How do you mean?"

"I suppose you're all driven by nobler drives."

"Who all? Teachers?"

"Like charity work isn't it? Poor buggers have no knowledge, so you give them some of yours."

"I suppose so … although they're not always as grateful."

"I bet. I bet. Ever had to do this before, Ivy?"

"Nope. Attendance is good normally."

"Never had anyone go missing?"

"Not while I've been there." Her ear was aching from pressing it to the receiver. Someone rang the doorbell. Ruth called to her again.

"Your friend Janette gave me a call yesterday." Janette – the school secretary, whose name she had forgotten.

"Really?"

"Said to cough up the boy or the police would be round."

"That's the next step, if we can't …"

"Didn't say to expect a call from you."

"She wouldn't have known; this was my idea."

"Aha! I thought so. Not part of the job description, to be a private spook."

"Ms Limms said something similar."

"What did I tell you? Knows me better than I know myself."

The door was answered and the hall filled with the commotion of many people greeting each other.

"So Carne is ill?"

"He told me you'd come searching for him too. Clever boy isn't he?"

"He is."

"He told me you were trying to make him your teacher's pet."

"Meaning what?" His illusiveness was irritating her.

"He's more than a pupil to you, that boy."

"Pardon me?" She gave a hurried wave to a bridesmaid poking her head around the door. Ruth shouted her name a third time.

"You called here hoping I'd solve all his secrets for you. Tell you if you kiss him he'll turn into a prince." His voice was stern and measured. Ivy could feel the skin of her cheeks warming. She searched frantically for something to say. "But he's a beast and you cannot fix him. He's mine and I know. I can tell you're a good woman, but don't try to love him. He's a beast."

"How can you … He's not a beast."

"He told me you'd say that. He said you believe in him so stubbornly. And who wouldn't? I bet it would be wonderful to save him. If anyone could save him, it would be you Ivy, but he's a beast."

"When will Carne be back in school?"

"Find someone else to rescue."

The doorbell rang again and she slammed the phone down.

24

Hokey cokey

THE STEPS CLUNKED UNDERNEATH her as she trotted up to the bridge and safety. Up here the moonlight was unobscured by treetops and the view of the open cityscape eased the claustrophobia. Ivy shivered, not quite from the cold. The trees she'd been walking through still murmured with the wind and cast confusing patterns on her path. At the middle she stopped and peered over the railings at the snaking blackness passing below. She was too high up to hear the currents. Ivy clasped the cold metal by her ribs, leaning her upper body over inch by inch. The thoughts were coming now, the ones she had been planning all the way up the steps. She let the first one in, it was half a thought and half a wish and it was cold like the bottom of the river. They didn't all come with words; they were not whole thoughts, just building blocks, not enough to make sense of if she ever remembered them again. The next was about Milo. Each bit of him she had fallen in love with continuing without her. The wind and the distant hum of traffic paused and she heard the river, rushing far below like deep electric static. One more – this one was for Milo too. It was made of the sounds of the river, but muffled and close and urgent. It had no words but *I hope,* spoken in a whisper at the back of her mind, barely audible above the gnashing current and Milo's bubbling breath. Indulgent thoughts, but she forgot them all …

She forgot them all in the warmth of the metal as it softened into wood, clammy from her sleepy hands. Her cheek was pressed against a numb forearm, her feet folded together under the chair. The classroom was dark. With a groan she levered herself up and wiped the drops of saliva from the open exercise book in front of her. The opposite wall flashed for a moment – a car's headlights illuminating thirty monster drawings pinned to the display board. Antennas and slime and triangular teeth. In here her thoughts were even smaller, just a little scratching in a faraway wall. She made out a shape in the gloom. He was sitting at the back in his usual seat – hunched and bony. Ivy closed the book. "I've been searching all over for you."

"They've been hiding me," he replied.

"What's wrong with you?" He scraped his chair along the floor as his only answer. "I wish I understood you, Carne … As whatever you are."

He lowered himself down and approached her. The shadows concealed all but the jagged bends of his limbs. She put her hand down to touch him as he scuttled towards her knees.

She came round in a blast of pop music. Ruth was plonked on her lap, white frills puffing up, with a glass poised on Ivy's lips. "Come back to us! And drink this! I can't remember what it is, I have to know! Taste it!" She tipped the glass too far and yelped as they both fought to catch the spills. "Ah, you look so beautiful and I'm ruining you." Ruth passed the glass to her sister. It was sugary and pungently alcoholic. "You're always the one to pass out. Learn to control yourself lady! I need your sisterliness."

"Sorry." The gulps she took were bringing her back to the room and numbing her premature hangover.

"Someone needs to be here to slow me. If I get too drunk I'll have a sloppy wedding night."

They were sitting at a table beside the dance-floor. A group of relatives danced in a circle ahead of them, arms linked, yelping as they kicked their legs in a ramshackle hokey cokey. Beyond them various couples swung each other back and forth, occasionally colliding. Their father bounced between groups, shouting and slapping people on the back. The table next to them was filled with the groom's brothers and friends, singing along to the music with their hands in the air and around each other. The room was bathed in purple light and beams of silver.

"I don't believe I fell asleep!"

"Ivy, the night wouldn't be complete without your customary nap."

"But it's your wedding."

"Shut up and drink, Grandma!" Ivy took another slug and

straightened herself up. "Am I crushing you?"

"It's ok, I was just sliding down the chair."

"Is the music ok? I was trying to get it cheesy, but not so cheesy that I alienate the men."

Ivy gestured to the table next to them. "The men look fine."

"Yea, they are some fine looking men. Yo! Men! My sister said you-lookin'-fine!" The nearest of the group sang in their direction. "You! Come and talk to my sister!" She stood up, steadying herself by grabbing his wrist, then yanked him out of his seat. "You're big aren't you? Ivy, come and speak to this large man."

Ivy stood up, making a show of reluctance.

Ruth put an arm around both of them. "Are you a surgeon too? Tell her about cutting people."

The man stumbled backwards into the table singing: "SURGURY! SURGURY! NA! NA!"

Ruth snatched Ivy by the arm and briskly led her away. "Greg's friends are such apes!" she said as they fought their way onto the dance floor.

Ivy twirled around trying to shake it off – that last trace of unease. Something murky clung to her, like a job needing done that hangs over a weekend. She rifled through her memories but found nothing, no real worries. Putting one hand on Ruth's shoulder she downed the rest of the glass and half gagged as the hokey cokeyers collided with them and bundled them in for the next dance.

25

Interrogation

ROAN SAT ACROSS FROM HER, searching for any sign that she recognized him. The room was empty but for the chairs and table. The ceiling hung low, enclosing them together in white. He traced back to that morning, the night before, the day before that, trying to work out how he came to be here and when he had slipped from reality. Getting to the hospital, the conversations in the dark, Pepper at his house admiring his paper city, all these days locked inside waiting to be seen, and now her. He needed his dream journal; that would set things right. He had not gone mad enough to believe this – his dead wife sitting across the table, about to interrogate him. And yet what else was there to believe?

Her hair was tightened in a ponytail, but it was still blonde, still curly. Her freckles had faded somewhat. There was a brisk formality to her manner that put him ill at ease. She wore a grey suit with a small emerald green brooch in the shape of a lizard. Roan soaked in the changes. When she sipped her coffee she made a different sound. It wasn't her. How could it be?

"I left you waiting here. I apologize. I don't like making people wait. It makes them worried. I hope you're not worried, Roan?"

He pulled his chair in, so his chest touched the table. "A bit, yes."

"You understand what you've been accused of?"

"Yes."

"We needed a while to do our research. You've been a stranger to us. No criminal record. Never arrested. And yet we asked around and people knew of you. Roan the street mime. Roan the eccentric. Roan the knight…" She stopped as though expecting an answer. He grunted. "The people we spoke to… they used to know you, or they know of you by name or sight, but we were hard pressed to find somebody close to you… You have a lot of secrets, Roan. I can see them in the way you look at me and in the stifled way that you speak. But that doesn't make you a murderer."

This was all his fault. He had allowed himself to teeter on the edge of sanity, peeking over the brink – a dirty kind of curiosity. The whole time he'd been thinking, *I'm not mad yet; I can find my way back.* And he still could. "You don't think I'm a murderer," he announced loudly.

She seemed intrigued by his sudden bravado. How had he won her love to begin with? That intrigued look, saying – *I want to work you out* – he remembered it. But it was gone again and he was back in the room with a stranger.

"How many friends do you have Roan?"

"It's hard to keep up with people…"

"Ten? …Twenty? …No? Ok, how many? You don't have to give me an exact number, just roughly?"

"I don't know."

"Roan we haven't even got onto the hard questions."

"I don't see a lot of the people I used to be friends with."

"Ok, so how many do you see?"

"Not many."

"How many?"

"None I suppose. Apart from…"

"Let me help you. You are friends with Peter Hansel, or Pepper."

"Yes."

"So the answer is one?"

"… Yes."

She had never mocked him like this; she'd always accepted his solitude. What had changed? She pressed her lips together. "So I'm guessing you enjoy your time alone then?"

"Yes."

"What do you like about it?"

"It's just what I'm used to."

"Have you ever been happy, Roan?"

A stray hair had come loose from her ponytail; he wanted to tuck it back in for her. He shifted around in his seat to face the corner of the room. Now she sat at the edge of his vision, where he was used to seeing her and where she was still a thought that had grown too strong. This relaxed him. It was just what he had wished, for her to come to his rescue and she had. He had been in the pitch black, talking to a beast. Now he sat in the fluorescent glare, speaking to the woman he loved. He answered her question in the affectionate tone he kept only for her. "Of course, I've been happy."

"When?"

"When we were married."

"Tell me about that, Roan."

"What is there to tell? You know all the answers."

"Describe a moment to me."

"All the time we were together, I was happy."

"A moment. One moment. Not the whole time. Describe to me a moment."

"Well …" Roan filtered through his memories. "Our wedding day."

"Come on. Don't be naff. You chose to get married, why?"

"Because we were in love.

"And you were happy when you were in love?"

"Exactly."

"So you were happy before your wedding day?"

"Yes."

"So describe to me a moment, an example of your happiness."

"Well there isn't any one moment. Or there was, but I can't think of one on the spot."

"That's unusual. Normally people have a moment that they love to play over and over in their minds and tell every poor sod who's willing to listen. Did you argue a lot?"

"Hardly at all."

"Tell me about an argument." He floundered again. "You can't describe either an up or a down?"

She stood up and strolled around the table. Roan turned around further, to keep her in the right place. From here there was no stern expression, just his familiar calm companion. "No kicking down doors? No drama? Fights? Rescues? Things a knight would do …"

Why had she kept this to herself for so long? Couldn't she have told him, if she wasn't happy? "I was happy, I didn't know that you …"

"Forget me, Roan, this is about you."

"How could I forget you?"

"I know it's hard. But try to be open with me; it's the best thing you can do. Does it bother you that you don't have a moment?"

"I didn't know love was supposed to be like that."

"Why won't you look at me, Roan?"

His control was fading in and out. One moment he was a husband, now a detainee, now a murderer. Where had the guilt come from the other day when he spied on that couple? What was he really watching them for? His throat was getting tight and he spoke with difficulty. "I was wishing you'd come … and you came," he said, willing her to be his wife again. "You have to help me out of this. I don't know how I got this far."

"Just be open and tell the truth and your co-operation will go a long way … Why did you go to the Hospital that night?"

"I just went for a walk and ended up there."

"Did you know there were other people there on the same night?"

"No."

"Did you hear anything? Or speak to anybody?"

Roan held back a stammer. "No."

"How many times have you gone to the Hospital?"

"I don't know."

"More than one?"

"A few. I walk a lot and sometimes I end up there."

She sat down in her chair again. He sneaked a glance and turned back to the wall. "You're being distant with me, Roan."

"I'm sorry. I can't help it."

"What made you so … faraway?"

"I never meant to be distant from you. I get lost in my mind. It doesn't change the way I feel."

"It seems a strange contrast that you make a living from having people look at you. And yet you find it so difficult to engage with them. You went to drama school, didn't you?"

"You know I went to drama school."

"You were an actor. And now you're a knight … Why are you a knight?"

"Simple stories. Happiness. Heroes."

"Do you feel heroic, Roan?"

"No."

"So you make a living dressed as a knight in shining armour in order to express that you're not a knight in shining armour. Is that the point?"

He sneaked another look and wished he didn't. It was not her. So many differences: the bone of her nose was more prominent, more redness in her cheeks and a lower hairline. Perhaps he had finally gone mad. "That's acting," he said bitterly.

"Do you miss her?"

"Every day."

"Roan, you have a house filled with letters that she wrote to you. And you've folded them to create what I'd call a paper town, or even a city. And inside it are little paper people."

"And?"

"The people are all in pairs."

"They are."

"I wonder how it would be to live in a city built of love letters. Peaceful I should think. I bet a lot of people would rather live that life than this, wouldn't they?" He coughed and shook to unlock the tension in his muscles. "Where did you learn origami?"

"I taught myself."

"You must have put a lot of time in … How long have you spent folding love letters?"

"I've no idea."

"Roughly. How many hours?"

Roan's mouth was gritty. He directed his answer to her lizard brooch. "I'm not good at keeping track of time."

"Funny you should say that … During my homework I found out something interesting about you. You are able to put yourself in a state of waking sleep. A state that allows you to stand for hours on end without being fully conscious. It's a remarkable skill. Must come in very useful in your job, for killing time."

"I couldn't do my job without it."

"Can you walk in this state?"

"Yes."

"Do you remember what it's like after it's over? Do you remember what you did?"

"Some ... Yes."

"Yes? Or sometimes?"

"Yes. Always."

"We've read your dream diary."

"Have you?"

"You see, I know you Roan. I know the answer to every question I ask."

"I know you do," he replied, smiling weakly.

"The people in your paper city, did you give them names?"

"No."

"Would you like to know their names?"

"What do you mean?"

"Would you like to know the names of all the people you've put inside your paper city?" She took a sheet from her pocket and unfolded it. *"Elliot Burns and Sandra Winslow, Naomi Duffman and Callum Campbell."* Roan chewed the inside of his mouth and wiped his palms against his trousers. *"Isa Andrew and Baby Edwin, Jennifer Streeks and Guy Tolmay. Milo Blakely and ..."*

"What's going to happen to me?"

"Do you understand what you've done, Roan?"

That guilt again, seeping in and saturating him, leaking down from a place he dared not look.

26

An intruder

THE BATHROOM WAS LIT by a single torch. It caught each particle of mist, making them gleam like fine dust. Ivy stood under the shower as they floated around her. The power had cut. It was Sunday night and work loomed heavy in the morning. She hadn't slept well all weekend, nor had she spoken to anyone. Going to bed would take her to tomorrow all the sooner, but what else was there to do? She stood there idly, waiting for the heat of the water to make her drowsy. Afterwards she patted her skin dry and moisturised her body in front of the long mirror. The torch beam made her slimmer and whiter and stretched the shadows on her face.

An idea came to her, a foolish one. Before there was time to doubt, she rifled through her clothes to find her phone and dialled the name at the top of her list.

"Hello?"

"Aaron. Can you hear me?"

"Ivy. What's up?"

Should she say it? "I think there's someone in my house."

Aaron arrived in ten minutes, gravely concerned. She beckoned him in, still wrapped in the towel, damp strands of hair clinging to her neck. He put a finger to his lips, straightening up to listen. "Where are they?"

"I don't know," she whispered back, as he widened his shoulders and took a slow step past her into the hall. He snooped from room to room holding her torch. He must have felt manly, with her huddling behind him touching the back of his jacket. But the image was breaking slowly with every room they visited. Every chair he accidently kicked made him less heroic. If there really had been an intruder, what a joke of a person to call.

"No one's going to fit in there," she said as he cautiously opened the dishwasher.

Still, what a help it was to have another familiar body next to her, even a fat and bumbling one. Soon it was clear that nobody was hiding in the house and they returned together to the kitchen table. She watched him as he lit a row of candles. How happy a damsel in distress had made him.

"I feel like an idiot now," she said as they sat down opposite each other.

"You shouldn't. You did the right thing."

"Really?"

"Well, yes."

"Shouldn't I have called the police?"

"Or that too. Maybe that would have been better. Ha."

"But, I called you."

"Well … luckily my ninja training wasn't put to the test." She didn't laugh – he did a bit, to cover the silence. "So how have you been?" he asked at last.

"Not good."

"No?"

"No … I'm not sleeping well."

"Oh? How come?"

"Work, stress, bad dreams."

"Yea. You work too hard."

She dipped her little finger in the hot wax. "Maybe … but I don't think it's that."

"Really?"

"… You got here quickly."

"Yea, you scared me. I was probably speeding."

"Probably? I should think so." She smiled at him, rolling the shell of wax onto the table. Her skin was still shiny from the lotion. His eyes sunk into her whenever she looked away. "You came to the rescue."

"Ha. Yea. A fat lot of good it did, but …"

"Aaron to the rescue … I'd feel more like an idiot if I'd called the police."

"It's better to be safe though, I suppose."

"You know me well enough to know I'm not going mad."

"Maybe a little." He made a clumsy wink.

"A little mad, or you know me a little?"

"Both?"

"You don't look at me like I'm mad." The candles flickered.

"You're in the top ten sanest people I've ever met."

"Thanks … Although if all your friends are like Milo, that's not saying much."

"No. I don't know anyone else like him, thankfully."

"You live half an hour away." She flicked a finger through the flame.

"Yea?"

"But you got here in ten minutes."

"Did I?"

"You knew I needed you."

He sat there without mystery, without poise, stunted by indecision. "It's easier when the roads are clear. At night."

"Were you in bed when I called?"

"No … not quite."

"You didn't come in your pyjamas?"

"Ha … no, I hadn't got changed."

"Oh …"

"It was no trouble."

"I don't like showering in an empty house," she said, just above a whisper. "It gives me the creeps."

"Yea, especially in the dark." Her hand was close enough to touch, if he wanted to.

"You should be here for every power cut."

"Maybe I should."

She hoped their eyes would stay locked, but he broke away. She gave him a few more seconds, knowing she would resist nothing, no matter how tentative or clumsy. But nothing came.

"I'm going to get dressed," she said and left the room. He didn't follow her. And as she sat on the bed brushing the tangles from her hair, the door stayed closed. When she had waited long enough, she dressed and descended the stairs. He was standing at the bottom, his jacket back on.

"I should probably to get going."

They hugged each other and he held her a little tighter than usual. She stayed in the doorway till long after he'd driven away.

27

Between here and home

"YOU ALWAYS LEAVE EARLY!"

"I know, I'm a sad old lady."

"Come back to us!"

She waved again and dipped through the tables towards the exit. Outside, the night air was crisp and ripe with cigarette smoke. It was a long way to walk, but that suited her mood.

Two police cars screeched past, spinning blue light over the crowded pavement. Ivy sped up to overtake a group of tottering girls and a bald man singing with a kebab and further past the line of bars and clubs, until the crowds began to thin. Tonight the alcohol had done nothing but make her sloppy and quiet. In the hope that the next drink would free her, she had continued until she could bear the company no longer.

"Hey there." A man in a shiny shirt sprung along beside her. She ignored him. "Why you walkin' so fast."

"I want to get home."

"I like a girl with a spring in her step."

"If you like me, then leave me in peace."

"Hey, I'm a peaceful guy, I'm a monk." His lines were snappy and flat, perhaps from overuse.

"You don't look like a monk," she replied, not sure why she was humouring him.

"Yea, I'm undercover."

"Ok."

"Hey, want to go watch a movie?"

"No thanks."

"Dinner?"

"No."

"Drink?"

"No."

"Walk in the park?"

"I'm ok."

"Ice cream." Ivy sighed. "Turkish delight? Ice skating? Climb a tree? Haha. Hey what's your name?"

"Please!" she implored.

"… Someone's upset you. Hope it wasn't me."

"What makes you say that?"

He studied her and gave a nod so small it was barely noticeable. "Have a good night." He turned to walk back.

As she pressed on the liveliness of the night shrunk to a faraway buzz. She imagined Milo somewhere out in this wilderness, making his way between strangers' houses. Why was it that she felt closest to him when she was alone? The street lights were stifled by overgrown trees. She moved to the middle of the road where she could see her steps. Ruth had once told her if she stayed with him too long she'd be contaminated. She looked around at the boarded-up windows and graffiti – a few years ago she would never have left friends and drinks to make this lonely walk. Maybe it was too late for her.

This was not a safe place but she'd gone too far to turn around. Another siren sounded in the distance. Something rustled near her. She imagined her life ending somewhere between here and home and how nonsensical that would make everything. Caught by Ruth's idea, Ivy tried to remember herself as she had been before marriage and how it was to walk and speak and sleep easier.

There was a rumbling and a flood of light. She sidestepped to let the car pass. It did so, slowly while the driver leered at her bare legs. When it turned a corner she hesitated between the pavement and road. The pavement was brighter here so she returned to it. The row of houses gave way to a small expanse of woodland that led to the railway. She entered slowly. The concrete path was peppered with more graffiti. For a while there was no sound but the wind and the clip of her shoes. She passed a bench and an overflowing bin. The grass flickered. Each tree seemed a bit human till she was close enough to see how the shadows had fooled her.

Brambles clawed through the chain link fence that boarded the railway. This was the loneliest part of the walk. She had only passed here once before at this time of night. It had been during his first disappearance, a year into their marriage. When he returned all she could do was weep with gratitude, forgetting her planned anger and all her pride. It was embarrassing to think of the power he used to have – that clueless rain-beaten boy on her doorstep. She heard a train approaching from behind, the last one of the night. As it shot past she tried to make out any people in the blur, but it was too quick. It wound into the distance and over the bridge until it was a string of light and gone.

The moon tinged the air with green. She followed the tracks and came to the edge of the park. A small alleyway wound up to the foot of the bridge. A screeching tyre and raised voices, from somewhere far off. If she could make it to the bridge she would be safe. Over the river the streets were less unsettling and her house was not much further. A breeze whisked around her neck and thighs. The path in the alley was sticky and the graffiti here was wildest. Ahead of her something stirred. A figure spinning around and crouching on the ground or just a trick? She stepped forward steadily and saw it was a branch, torn and hanging from its trunk. The slightest wind made it sway. It hung by a strip of bark, poised on the concrete floor, waiting to be torn free. Ivy looked back along the path then gripped the branch and yanked it. The ripping of the wood was louder than she expected. The branch was still attached and it creaked after her as she left it and quickened her pace.

At the foot of the bridge she stopped, glancing back again and up the stairs. For a moment she saw herself as if from outside – her made-up face ghoulish in the moonlight, her goose-pimpled flesh. How many people wandered out alone, thinking they were the only ones? Tipsy self-absorbed twenty-somethings leaving the pub early to take a lonely walk home. With a trot, she climbed the steps to the bridge and safety.

Even before she reached the top step she had it planned: she would walk to the middle and look downwards at the snaking blackness and reflected streetlights. She would spare a few more dark thoughts before heading home. Maybe she would wonder about jumping in

and how much further she would need to go before the bed of the
river was a cosier home than the one she had. She would think about
Milo and whether he felt that same tug of the riverbed. And when she
was done she would move on with a lighter tread. Indulgent thoughts.

But what she saw made her forgot them all.

28

A story's end

...IT WAS LIKE WALKING OVER SNOW and making no foot prints.
"Do I know this story?"

It crawled closer and craned its neck. *Don't you want to hear the ending?*

Roan lay curled up on the foam mattress, the stone beneath it pressing into his hip. It was well into the night. The metal grill on the door spared a few slivers of corridor light, just enough to give shape to the room. From outside came the sound of shuffles and grumbled monologues from other cells. There had been no great despair when the door clanged shut. Even now as the hours passed he was calm, the guilt had settled.

Roan watched it creep towards him and fold its jagged legs.

"Not right now."

It was his own creation, everything he imagined a monster to be: the contorted limbs, sinews twinging with inhuman life. He had dreamed it all up. So how could it speak with its own words? He sat up and edged forward, elbows supported on his crossed legs, bringing his nose towards it as close as he dared. There was a question on his mind that had been eating away at him. "Can you fly?" That wasn't it.

Of course. It remained crouched at his feet, choosing not to demonstrate. He wanted to touch it, to feel how solid his imagination really was. Not yet. He was formulating his next question when it spoke up.

Do you understand what you've done?

"I don't feel like a murderer."

How do you feel?

"Ok thanks."

Roan chortled at the absurdity of his own response and then again when he imagined ever trying to explain the joke to another human. What a serious word 'human' is, so intellectual and detached. "Hu-man! Hu-man! Hu-man! Hu-man!" he repeated until the meaning of the word unravelled. Somewhere in the repetition the words passed downward, leaving him silent while his companion chanted up at him. It sounded like an accusation. He imagined himself held up in front of a planet of these creatures, all chanting at him, pointing their twisted claws. It stopped. Roan searched for a moment of calm.

Why did you ask if I could fly?

"I was wondering."

I thought you would remember me.

Had that memory always been there? Being a child and wings above him, beating. Something infecting him, slowly driving everyone away. Something from above.

"Pepper put you here."

What else did Pepper do? it asked with a poisonous inflection, like anger and inhuman strength from the pit of Roan's belly. The feeling of having gone too far and burrowing deeper to escape.

Did Pepper put that there too?

The feeling passed. For a while the creature was insubstantial and meaningless, just a crooked prehistoric bird.

"Who was that woman yesterday?" he asked feebly, his palm already clasped inside the suit sleeve of the memory, climbing up around her warm wrist. Perhaps she would come back to him, open his cell door and tell him it was all a mistake. Or as he was wishing – why not come back a few steps further, knock on his bedroom door and sooth away this whole succession of nightmares. As he played out this fantasy he peered into its pale eyes. They held each other's gaze with the simple ease of knowing someone better than a friend or even a reflection. "Are we friends now?"

You won't need me much longer. The response was so measured, like a psychiatrist was speaking.

Again the irony made him snort. "I'm thinking of her and looking at you."

Close them if you prefer.

Another memory: his hand smoothing over eyelids, leaving them down. Eye lashes prickling against his fingers, a strange kind of intimacy. It came with a lurch and vanished again, leaving only her in his mind. Yesterday she had sounded so punchy and business-like. She couldn't have been more different and yet he would have fallen in love with her too, given half a chance. All the memories he replayed so greedily and still he couldn't think of one happy moment. Just scenes of walking side by side, trapped in separate minds. His touch and her being touched and the vastness in-between. And above him, in every memory, the shadow of wings. She could have been anyone, just homely and soft like a duvet to hide under when you hear voices in the night.

"Where's that story from?"

It's just a story. To help you sleep.

"I can't imagine ever sleeping again."

All that guilt, when I go I'll take it with me. And you'll understand what you've really done.

"What's that?"

They wanted to go where you took them. People here only saw them disappear. But you know what's on the other side. Over the edge of the world.

At last Roan asked his question. "What's it like to not be real?"

Let me tell you the end of the story. Its eyes closed with a crunch. Roan followed suit and listened in darkness.

The knight trod forwards over the white. A third step and a fourth. He waited, gripping his sword. But there was no swooping, no gnashing of teeth, just patient steps away from the shore. Behind him the people at the edge watched where he had gone. By the time he turned and made his way back they had all given up on the show.

The journey home was a quiet one. At night his dreams were simpler and less troubled. His hometown buzzed more faintly. When he rang the bells of houses he knew, strangers answered, looking half at and half through him. He went to sleep beneath a bridge, away from the wind, listening for beating wings.

For many years he lived like this. The thumping of his sword against his thigh reminded him he was still a knight even when his horse had gone. How much had the dragon grown since their last encounter? Asking this changed the way he listened: instead of scrabbling claws he listened for growls as deep as earthquakes and watched the sky for flickers in front of the moon. But when it came, it was not from above. He was dozing on the pavement beneath the bridge when he heard it, so faint it was not enough to make a memory.

The next night he heard it again – a breath like a receding wave. He had no bed to look under so he pressed his palm onto the ground. The paving stones were smooth and grey and diamond-shaped. With each breath they heaved up and down. He wriggled from his ragged sleeping bag and ran through the night. Everywhere he went the diamond grey paving stones breathed his footsteps up and down. He touched a shop front window – it was breathing too. The bonnet of a car – it was breathing too. The stars and moon and passing planes, they all rose and sank with gigantic sighs. In the middle of an empty road he drew his sword and plunged it into the ground with all his might. Underneath the grey shell it was soft like putty. The blade sank to the hilt and he yanked it back and forth, crunching through the scales. The breaths quickened and the ground welled up with blood as white as the pages of a storybook.

29

Crumpled

MILO AWOKE IN BED, below a clean white ceiling, unable to move. The graffiti, the mould, the disintegration, it was all gone. Nearby he heard the sound of hurried feet and conversations. A television was on somewhere, playing an old musical with squeaky jazz trumpets. The sheets and pillows smelled of cheap detergent. Two faces appeared over his bed from either side.

"You have overdosed, my man," said Isa. "But we are a hospital after all."

Milo tried to speak. A finger touched his lips and Baby shook her head.

"No talking. No moving. No thinking." His heart rate bleeped on a machine out of sight. She plugged a liquid into the drip above the bed. It slithered through the tube and into his hand.

Left alone again, Milo listened to the steady bleep from beside the bed. His heart was thumping satisfyingly in time. For a while he lay listening and feeling simultaneously, trying to detect mismatches, but there were none. He felt the coarseness of the bed sheets against his legs. The television was turned off. In the distance he heard an intercom and the slamming of doors. The bleep and the beat of his heart ran side by side until he believed they both came from him. He closed his eyes, thankful for the peace.

The thud of his heart was louder without the distraction of sight. He listened passively to what seemed like the drum of his judgement. The joy of regularity was back, the same joy he felt listening to a repetitive beat from a speaker. Despite his concentration he failed to notice when it happened: the bleep and the beat had separated. His heart thumped and in the pause the monitor bleeped – still in rhythm but not in time. Perhaps the machine had changed setting. Or were they even synchronised to begin with? He was too tired to wonder. Another change was coming. He noticed it straight away: *Bleep, thump, bleep bleep, thump, bleep, thump, bleep bleep, thump*. The sounds pounded through him. The next change came: *Bee-bee-bleep, thump, bleep bleep, thump, bee-bee-bleep, thump, bleep bleep, thump.* All around him the noises vibrated so loudly the inside of his ears tickled. *Bleep-beda-thump, beda-bleep-beda-thump, bleep-beda-thump, beda-bleep-beda-thump.*

It was like being welcomed home to see the dancing figures above him and the graffiti on the ceiling. He rose to his feet. Around him people flailed their bodies to the music. They seemed frail, as if the speakers were shaking them to pieces. Milo was frail too; as he moved even the air was buffeting against him until the ground barely touched his feet.

"Tip-toe-tip-toe-tip-toe-tip …?" said the voice in time to the beat.

From an empty window frame the moon shone, turning the city white. There was no rushing of blood, no dizziness; he was clean and empty. In the darkness he didn't notice her until she was inches away, her eyes aligned with his. They looked blacker than ever.

"Sylvie."

There was a lull as the bass faded out, ready to thunder back at the next drop. A breeze passed between them. She quivered. The moon went behind a cloud as the bass dropped in again and everyone turned to silhouettes. He reached to where he thought her hand was. It was cool and welcoming and the more he squeezed it the more it crumpled.

30

The bridge

HE WAS SITTING ON THE GROUND, bent forward in sleep or stupor. His arms leant limply on his knees. There was dirt smeared along his sleeves and under his nails, like he had been trying to dig a hole. Ivy crouched next to him, unsure where to place a comforting hand. She settled on a clean spot by his shoulder. He coughed, making his whole body jerk.

"What have you done to yourself?" He shivered and petted at her arm. "Can you walk?" He wriggled around and toppled forward onto his front. "What happened … ? Look at me."

He studied her, straining to recognise. "Miss?"

"I'm calling an ambulance."

"I'm fine. I'm not sick."

"It isn't safe, here."

"I'm fine."

"Come with me."

"I'm …" He dragged himself along beside her. "I'm not sick. Or hurt. I'm just sleepy." He spaced out his words. When he crawled he wobbled at the knees and elbows.

"That's not a good place to sleep." His mouth was twisted in a smile. One she had seen in other people. "Have you taken something?"

"Are you going to take me to Ms Lobo? HA!"

"Carne, that's not for children. You could really …"

"Fuck myself up?"

"Let's go." She crouched and took his arm awkwardly. He yanked it free and pulled his hood up. "Don't shut me out. I could have you in so much trouble, if I choose."

"With who?"

"The police. With school. With your parents. Where shall we start?"

He held the bottom of the railings and pulled himself along faster. They approached the steps on the other bank. Ivy cast a glance back to the steel archways of the bridge and the wilderness she'd walked through. Carne gripped the railings harder and lowered his first hand onto the stairs. She followed carefully, ready to jump to the rescue if he fell. His descent was slow and shaky. When they reached the pavement at the bottom he stretched and looked up and down.

"Why did you take me this side? I live on the other side."

"You want me to take you home like this?"

"No."

"Come with me then." The burden of moral dilemma had sobered her up. She paced on ahead with a military rhythm.

"Quick march. Two, three, four," Carne muttered next to her, padding the ground. "What's the rush? And where are we going?"

"I'm taking you to the police."

"What? Why?" He stopped and swayed to the side in surprise.

"I'm joking Carne. I'm taking you to my house, so you can clean up. Your Dad can't see you like this."

"Your jokes are shit."

"Well, lucky I became a teacher and not a comedian."

"Lucky you don't try to be funny in class."

As she slotted the key in her front door she quietly hoped Milo would not choose tonight to come back and beg forgiveness. Her young student slunk in behind her. The house was dark and didn't respond to her hellos. She switched on all the lights.

"Right you. Go to the bathroom and clean yourself up. It's to the left at the top of the stairs. Use the green towel on the rack opposite the toilet. Don't get mud on it. Go. Quick march!"

He shuffled towards the stairs. The last of the alcohol in her blood was easing out. She knew this would be a secret and she hated secrets. She laid out four slices of bread and went to the fridge for filling. The boiler droned as the shower ran upstairs. She chopped the cheese into two sandwiches and sat down at the table to eat.

Carne returned in the same clothes, with clear skin and ruffled wet hair. She pointed to the sandwich she had left for him. His bites were slow and uneven, as if he was just learning to chew. He held the sandwich, examining it.

"I haven't poisoned it."

"I know."

"Do you always stare at your food like that?"

"Sometimes."

Both sat listening to the other chewing and swallowing. Occasionally Carne looked up quizzically.

"What's funny?" she asked.

"You swallow really loudly. It's like *shhhcumofff*"

"I could say the same about you."

"You're worse. You sound like a swamp."

"Thanks."

"Do I sound like that too?"

"Your throat's smaller than mine. When you grow up it'll be louder."

"And I'll get hair growing from my nose and ears."

"Who told you that?"

"I don't need to be told."

"Maybe you will, but not till you're fifty."

"I'll never be fifty."

"Oh yes you will."

"I don't want to be."

"Well you shouldn't want to be fifty when you're eight. That would be weird. You're a slow eater today." Carne had managed only three bites, while Ivy polished off her last.

"Not normally."

"I hear it spoils your appetite."

"What does ...? Who did you hear that from?"

"Never you mind."

"Never I mind?"

"What else does it do?"

Carne studied her without blinking. "Can I have a drink?"

"Help yourself." He made his way to the fridge peering about the room curiously. "It certainly makes you look funny. Like you're interested in everything ... Maybe you should take it in school." Carne turned back to her from the open fridge and grinned. "I'm glad you know that was a joke." She fetched him a glass and he poured himself some milk. Suddenly he was such a boy.

"So ..." Ivy began carefully.

"I knew it."

"What?"

"I knew you would be all friendly. And then say ... *So Carne, what's really troubling you? Let's talk about it.*"

"What makes you think that?"

"Just talk normally. Don't treat me like a kid."

"But you are a ..."

"Pretend I'm not."

"Will that help?"

"It won't cos you can't."

"Just because you're cleverer than the others in class, that doesn't make you an adult."

"I've done everything you've done. And more."

"I'm not sure that's ..."

"Tell me something you've done."

"I was going to say I don't think that's relevant."

"You don't believe me."

"It doesn't matter if I believe you."

"How could it not matter? I'm in your house, so I trust you. You could be a paedophile. But I trust you. You should trust me."

"Ok, you're not a boy. You're a young man. Happy?"

"I'm not a man either. You don't understand though. You're trying to think of all the things I haven't done."

"I don't want to know what you've done."

"I'm not what you think I am."

"Oh no?"

"But you can pretend I'm a man."

"Carne, I ..."

"You can't," he was sitting bolt upright gripping the arms of the chair, his lips chapped and his skin deathly white. "You can't, because you know what I'd be doing to you, if I was a man."

"Your lip's bleeding." He sat back, sucking it, still watching her. "You're a strange one Carne."

"I'm going to tell you a secret," he said calmly.

"Carne, I don't want to hear it."

"I'm going to tell you because you won't believe it so it doesn't matter … I wasn't born like you were born."

"Carne."

"Ha! What did I tell you? You wouldn't believe me. Let's talk about whatever shit you wanted to."

"I can help you, if you let me."

"HA! HA! HA!"

"Carne don't laugh at me like that."

"Do you believe in witches?"

"This was a mistake. You need to go home."

"I was raised by witches."

"You're trying to scare me, when I brought you here to help you."

"You brought me here because you want me to open up to you. Well I'm opening up."

Ivy took a long unsteady breath and was about to speak when Carne sprung up on his two hind legs and circled the table towards her. She recoiled as he stepped next to her chair. His skinny little body leant forward towards her.

"Why are you scared of me? I'm just a boy," he said and slid his fingers down her hair and cheek and lips.

About the Author

Kit O'Conor is a British author whose debut novel *Tiptoe* was released in 2014. Since graduating in Philosophy at Southampton University, Kit has travelled extensively and worked in many fields from sales to English teaching. Currently he is living in London drafting his second novel. You can reach him through kitoconor.com, or follow him on Twitter @KitOConor.

Also by Kit O'Conor
Balloons

A sordid festival comes to a premature and devastating end, leaving the life of an adolescent boy changed forever. Many years later and he's shared the secret with no one, not his ailing father, his new wife, or even his cat. But just when it's nearly forgotten, the event he witnessed that day takes on a bizarre new significance. It all starts when he hears a voice inside the paving stones.

A haunting short story by the author of *Tiptoe*, available exclusively on Amazon Kindle.